~~Not~~ in the Christmas Plan

ETTA EASTON

Contents

Author's Note   1

1. Chapter 1   2

2. Chapter 2   8

3. Chapter 3   19

4. Chapter 4   28

5. Chapter 5   35

6. Chapter 6   42

7. Chapter 7   52

8. Chapter 8   61

9. Chapter 9   70

10. Chapter 10   75

11. Chapter 11   84

12. Chapter 12   96

13. Chapter 13   105

14. Chapter 14   113

15. Chapter 15   119

16. Chapter 16   125

17. Chapter 17   130

18. Chapter 18   135

19. Chapter 19   139

20. Chapter 20   147

21. Chapter 21   152

About the author   154

Also by Etta Easton   155

Author's Note

This book contains themes of parental loss, traumatic birth, and babies in the NICU. While the overall story leans toward joy, hope, and ultimately love, these moments may be difficult for some readers. I've done my best to approach them with care.

Please prioritize your emotional well-being as you read.

Etta <3

Chapter One

On all that is holy, if I had known Grant was going to gobble up all the pie, I would have bought a store made one just for him.

I watch him through narrowed eyes, shaking my head.

Look at him, up there being all greedy. He thinks he's slick, but I saw the way he looked at me before getting up for his third piece, and I know he's doing it on purpose. Going for as much as he can just to get a rise out of me. Never mind the other four adults here who might want some before he—

"Ouch!" I hiss as a sharp pain radiates from the back of my arm and glare at my sister. "Did you just pinch me?"

"Yes," Ivy whispers hotly. "And I'll do it again if you don't stop!"

"Stop what? All I'm doing is sitting here."

I rub my arm to soothe the sting away while pulling up a mental image of the cabinet she keeps her prenatal vitamins in. I know she needs them for the extra calcium and iron and everything, but if she uses those talons on me again, I'm tossing her vitamins right in the trash.

Ivy narrows her eyes in that 'you know exactly what I'm talking about' glare, and after a few seconds I drop my scowl for a pout.

"But that's his third slice!" I say, leaning into her so no one else hears my righteous complaint.

"So? You should take it as a compliment that someone actually likes your baking."

"First of all—rude. And second—compliment? He's only doing it to get under my skin. Didn't you see his smirk before he got up? He's being petty."

Ivy rolls her eyes. "Grant is the least petty person I know. Besides, you brought two pies, Eve. Stop being stingy and let the man eat."

"But—"

"No buts. You promised me."

Ivy's solemn reminder has me biting the inside of my cheeks.

I made a promise to be nice to the man, yes, but that was before I knew he was a pie thief.

It took me three baking sessions, peeling six pounds of potatoes, overcooking two pies, under cooking one, and fighting back tears while trying to correctly roll out crust, all to get my sweet potato pies to look and taste just like Dad's. I thought everyone understood that in the Matthews household, we don't touch dessert until dinner's done and the Christmas season officially begins with a movie. Everyone, apparently, except for Grant, who dug right in as soon as the last bite of mac and cheese had been scraped off his plate.

"Furthermore," I continue, because forget my promise. I'm mad all over again thinking of my disregarded hard work. "He didn't even use the whipped cream I bought. Don't you remember how I told you somebody's auntie tried to straight up take it out of my basket?"

"*Eve*." Ivy's exasperated tone is unmistakable, along with her those pleading eyes. "Please."

Ugh. And I know what that 'Please' means. Please, make this Thanksgiving easy on her. It's her first hosting her in-laws, including her brother-in-law, Grant. Her first eating for three. And our first without Dad's booming laughter echoing in our childhood home.

My chest squeezes, but before thoughts of how much I miss Dad can take root and intrude on what should be a day of thankfulness, I lower my gaze and focus on Ivy's belly. AKA, the other reason I capitulated to Grant coming over and my being nice to him. Ivy's pregnant. Like, *really* pregnant. Her stomach is so swollen that her chair is pushed back at least a foot more than mine, and she looks ready to pop. She actually looked ready to pop about three months ago, not that I'd ever admit that out loud.

"I'm serious," Ivy presses at my silence. "Do not make me have to go off on you and embarrass both of us in front of Braxton's parents."

And people say I'm the mean twin.

"Fine," I huff out. "I'll be nice. Just like I promised."

"What are you two whispering about over there?" Wardell, Ivy's father-in-law asks us from his seat at the end of the table.

Ivy attempts to reposition herself to face him, but all she does is wobble back and forth for a few seconds. In the end she gives up and simply turns her head in his direction.

"Oh, you know, just twin things," she answers breezily before leaning back in her seat, though she looks far from relaxed. Despite her glowing skin, her eyes droop with exhaustion and her mouth pulls at the corners.

"Anyone else want a piece while I'm up?" Grant asks from his spot at the counter, *standing over the pie*, with a knife in his eager hand.

"Not until we start the movie," Ivy and I say at the same time.

"Copy!" I rush out before Ivy can.

"Darn it," she says with a tired laugh. "Paste."

"Another twin thing?" Wardell asks and Ivy and I laugh in unison.

The 'Copy, Paste' thing came from Dad. He loved three things: his daughters, his sports teams, and his computers. He owned a computer repair shop downtown and taught computer literacy at the rec center with heart and humor. I am helplessly lost when it comes to all things sports, but get me in front of a crowd and I can spout out some of his computer jokes at the drop of a dime.

What's a computer's favorite snack? Microchips!

How does a computer get drunk? By taking screenshots!

Whenever Ivy and I would blurt out the same thing at the same time, he'd go about calling us Copy and Paste for the next hour. Though we've always loved our twinhood, for two kids trying to assert our individuality, Paste felt like an insult we had to avoid at all costs, and so we made a game of it.

"I wonder what little inside games these two will cook up," Ivy says to me, rubbing her belly and letting me know her thoughts are along the same path as mine.

Her mouth tightens and a small V forms between her eyebrows. Before I can ask if she's okay, I'm distracted by Grant.

He's back in his seat directly across from mine, humming a surprisingly decent falsetto of Patti LaBelle's "If Only You Knew" as he closes his eyes and chews.

The man is so unserious. This is the third time he's busted out in song after taking the first bite of a new piece.

His thick eyebrows lift as his face twists with soulful emotion. Full lips purse inward and the tip of his tongue peeks through as if devouring every last bit of flavor.

When he opens his eyes and his gaze meets mine, playful and taunting, I'm the first one to look away.

Yup, unserious.

Ivy lets out a pained moan, and all heads swivel to her.

"Are you okay, Baby?" Braxton asks, leaning toward his wife and placing his hands on top of hers.

My adrenaline spikes in the moments it takes Ivy to catch her breath and for her shoulders to relax.

"I don't know. I started having contractions a few hours ago and was waiting—" She stops and shuts her eyes on another wave of pain. "I was waiting to see if they would go away with some food and water. They seem to be getting stronger, but this is too early to go into labor. Right?"

Go into labor? Now? Oh my God, oh my God! Begins running on a loop through my mind as I stare at Ivy's stomach. Her stomach where two whole babies are about to try and bust out from. Now. Today. *Oh my God!*

Ivy turns to me, her brown eyes full of fear and pain, and I know I need to keep it together for her. No panicking.

I went into full research mode when she told me she was carrying twins, wanting to be able to help her every step of the way. Most doctors consider thirty-seven weeks full-term for twins. Ivy just hit thirty-five, so while it's still early, it's not uncommon. Twins often come earlier. Ivy and I came at thirty weeks.

When a voice in my head points out how we were the only ones who made it out of the hospital while our mom didn't, I drown it out and quickly stand up. "This is it, everyone! Operation Womb-Mates is on."

Chapter Two

"**I**'ve got the go-bag!" I shout. "Braxton, Mr. Wardell, help Ivy to the car." I nod at Ivy's mother-in-law. "Mrs. Linda, you're on brownies for the nurses. Second shelf in the freezer. Go! Go! Go!"

Everyone has a role to ensure Ivy gets to the hospital safely and without delay. We got together on Halloween, and between passing candy out to adorable trick-or-treaters, we ran through every possible scenario—if she went into labor home alone, in the middle of H-E-B, or while Braxton was stuck in traffic on I-35. So while this is unexpected, it's also a bit serendipitous that we're all here together.

En masse, chairs scrape against hardwood in a frenzy.

I back away from the table, scanning the controlled chaos, and wince. *Almost* everyone has a role. Halloween was one of the few gatherings Grant hadn't crashed, which means he wasn't part of the plan. Now he's rocking on the balls of his feet looking eager to jump in, but I don't have the time to delegate or worry about him. I need to focus on Ivy.

I press my lips together and turn away.

"Let's get moving, people!" I call, sprinting for the coat closet.

Ivy's gym bag is right where it should be, bursting at the seams with fuzzy socks, a soft robe, a few books, her bonnet, and about a dozen other comfort items. When I pick it up and spin around, Braxton and his dad are supporting Ivy on either side as they make their way to the cars in the garage.

Ten feet away from the door, Ivy gasps.

"Wait!" She looks at Braxton with wide eyes. "I don't have my shoes on."

"Shoes?" Braxton's face goes blank then slack with horror as he looks down at her bare, purple painted toes to the empty space on the shoe rack where the only shoes she can fit these days would be. "Where'd they go?"

Ivy's chin trembles. "I don't know!"

"Okay, okay. What about socks?" Braxton suggests. "The thick ones you kept asking for last week because you liked the way they made your ankles look are in the drawer. I'll run and get them for you."

Before Braxton can take off, Ivy's body nearly folds in half as a contraction rocks her, but she still manages to pant out, "I'm not showing up to the hospital in Frankenstein socks when it's nearly Christmas."

"Baby, you're in labor. I don't think the doctors and nurses care about your feet matching the season. You can show up with them stuffed inside turkeys and no one will bat an eye."

It's evident Braxton's chosen the wrong time to crack jokes when Ivy's arm snakes up, clutching his shirt and dragging him down to her level. "You don't understand. I need shoes. Not socks, not *turkeys* or whatever else you're thinking of suggesting. Shoes on my feet, or these babies stay in me!"

My sweet, level-headed sister has left the building.

Braxton gulps. "Yes. Shoes. Got it. Uh, here, t-take mine!"

When not full of pregnancy hormones and pain, Ivy loves her some Braxton. She'd be devastated if he missed the birth of their babies because he was busy getting stitches.

Good thing I'm here.

I step forward. "Don't worry, I'll find—"

"Got the shoes!" Grant shouts from another room.

Two seconds later, he rushes from around the corner, stopping in front of Ivy to ease her feet into fur-lined clogs.

Feet covered and cozy, Ivy visibly relaxes and looks up at Braxton with eyes docile as a doe while she smooths his shirt.

"Crisis averted," Grant says, standing up and dusting his hands on his dark jeans.

Grant's a handsome guy, *if* you're into tall ex-NBA players who've kept their fit physique, with deep brown skin and even deeper brown eyes that carry the kind of warmth you'd expect from a mug of hot chocolate.

Which, of course, is ridiculous. No one's eyes should make a person feel like curling up by the window and forgetting the world.

Okay, the man is fine with a capital F, bolded and underlined.

He smiles tenderly at Ivy, brushing a kiss on her forehead, then claps Braxton on the shoulder with an encouraging, "You got this, bro."

When his eyes meet mine, I swear there's a spark of triumph before he looks away.

I barely hold in my scoff. As if finding a pair of shoes or hyping his brother up like *he's* the one about to push two babies out of him makes Grant the hero of the day.

I shift the go-bag to my other arm and open the door to the garage, keeping it wide so Braxton and his dad can get through with Ivy.

Braxton pulls on the passenger's handle, only to throw his head back with a groan. "I forgot my keys."

"Got 'em," Grant says, jingling a set of keys with a Dallas Cowboys keychain above his head. "Got your wallet, too."

With the flick of his wrist, Grant aims the key fob at the car and the sharp click of doors unlocking bounces off drywall.

Well, whoopty doo. He's got some special knack for finding exactly what people need.

I grit my teeth and watch Braxton guide Ivy down into her seat. Once the seatbelt is stretched safely over her belly and Braxton is making his way to the driver's side, I move in, "accidentally" bumping Grant out of my way. It may be petty of me, but the surprised grunt he lets out is satisfying.

The dip in my stomach from his heated glare, however, is uncalled for.

"It's not too early, right?" Ivy asks when I'm back at her side.

"It's not too early."

"And everything's going to be fine?"

"Everything will be fine," I say, channeling calm confidence. I run a hand over her jeweled locs while holding her gaze. "You've got your hair nice and fresh, so you won't have to worry about looking cute while pushing out my nieces."

She laughs and shakes her head. "I am not worried about how my hair looks. Just my feet."

"You've got your go-bag with everything to keep you comfy. And your husband by your side."

A glance up shows me an eyes-wide-with-panic Braxton receiving a similar pep talk from Grant.

"You got this," Grant says. "And remember, if she says anything mean during labor—don't take it personally."

The door leading inside opens and Braxton's mom comes running out. "The brownies are ready!"

She rushes to jump into the backseat with a wrapped box of brownies and a tag with the words 'Thank you, nurses' written across.

Because of hospital restrictions, it was decided that Linda and Wardell would accompany the new parents to the hospital, and I would be able to come after the birth. I don't like it, but Braxton's parents treat Ivy like their own, so I know she'll be in good hands.

Braxton and his dad load into the car as well and with final nervous goodbyes, they back out.

My little sister, my twin, is about to have her own set of twins.

As the car disappears from view, cold November air sweeps into the garage, passing right through my thin sweater. I wrap my arms tightly around my body, but it barely stops the chill and does absolutely nothing for the sudden hollow feeling that settles over me. Ivy and I were supposed to be doing this together.

From the time we were young girls, we'd imagined doing life side by side—marriage, babies, family holidays—and having our kids grow up more like siblings than cousins. For a while, it even looked like it would happen. Ivy had Braxton, who was loyal and ready to build his life around her. And I had Eddie, who I thought was equally as loyal, until Grant showed me photographic proof that shattered everything.

I should probably worship the ground Grant walks on for saving me from a lifetime of regret, but if there's one thing I've learned as a family lawyer, it's that emotions don't always allow us to do what's logical. Emotions are messy. They make you act out or collapse into yourself, run from the people you love or cling too tightly, do everything you possibly can to keep from hurting any more.

Especially when grief is involved.

And shortly after breaking things off with Eddie, I lost Dad.

Life went on, it always does, and I kept working cases and trying to be there for Ivy while she planned her wedding, knowing the man who meant the most to both of us wouldn't be there to walk her down the aisle.

It was during one of those wedding-prep days when everything finally caught up with me. It'd been just Grant and me assembling dozens of tiny Lego figurines for Ivy and Braxton's wedding favors. Grant was trying to cheer me up with jokes and offering peppermints from a stash in his pocket he must have taken from someone's grandma. What I probably needed was a hug, but when he dangled that crinkly wrapper in my face, I went in for a kiss.

Admittedly, I'd always felt a pull to him—one I ignored while planning a future with Eddie—but in that moment, there was nothing to hold me back.

The instant our lips touched though, I knew it was a mistake. No man on this earth had a right to possess lips that soft, that sweet, that alluring. One kiss and I'd been tempted to throw all my troubles on Grant and let him carry them away. I wanted to give up all control when I'd already lost so much.

When he tried to discuss the kiss like emotionally stable adults and made it clear that he wanted to give *us* a chance, I told him it was a mistake. I pulled back not only from the kiss, but also the friendship we'd built in the orbit of Ivy and Braxton. It was the only way I knew to protect myself. Months later, it still is.

The garage door shuts, sealing us in silence. I drag myself out of the past, leaving behind everything beyond my control, and force my attention back to the present, which honestly is no better.

With everyone gone to the hospital it's only Grant and me here.

He's on the other side of the garage, standing there with arms crossed over his chest, feet planted on the concrete, and a faraway look in his eyes. Does he realize that this is the first time since the kiss we've been alone?

I suck in a cleansing breath. I need something else to focus on. "I'm going to clean the kitchen," I announce, already halfway to the door.

The sink is full, counters crowded, and table full of half-eaten meals. I roll up my sleeves and get to work. I dig out Tupperware and Ziplock bags and begin packing the turkey, greens, and Linda's chitlins gravy.

Funny thing about that—I've spent all of my twenty-eight years living in the South, having grown up here in Bliss, Texas and moved to San Antonio after school—but have never had chitlins until today.

Dad used to tell us how Mom loved them, but he couldn't stomach the smell. She'd insist on cooking them anyway, and he'd insist she leave the front and back doors open, as well as all of the downstairs windows. I wonder what would have happened if he'd been here when Linda proudly walked in with her pot of gravy, eager for Ivy and me to try it? Dad had a good poker face, so I'm sure he would have smiled and offered to take it off her hands.

Then "accidentally" poured the whole thing down the sink while the garbage disposal was on.

I fight back the lump in my throat. It was so unfair that a car accident took him from us when Ivy needed him to guide her through her new role as a wife, and I needed him in the aftermath of my heartache.

I've spent the past year trying to heal, but sometimes I can't help but wonder what else will be taken from me.

Suddenly I'm cramming food into the fridge with no methodical care. Turkey smothers the eggs, the pan of green beans balance on the rolls. A lid slips, clattering to the floor and I freeze, realizing my hands are trembling.

"No," I whisper, too quiet for anyone else to hear.

Everything is fine. Ivy's fine. The babies will be fine. Nothing bad is going to happen. Especially not during Christmas.

The sound of Grant moving in the living room reaches me, reminding me that I'm not alone. And the last thing I want is for him to see me fall apart.

I take in a long breath. Then another. Then my gaze lands on the table. Among nearly finished, abandoned plates sits one covered by a paper towel—Grant's slice of pie. I don't know why, but something about seeing it there just sets me off.

I pick it up and carry it to the trash.

Grant walks in just as I hold the plate over the can. "Hey, I'm still eating—"

The pie slides off and lands with a dull plop.

I meet his eyes, feigning innocence. "I'm sorry, did you still want that?"

Grant narrows his eyes. "Guess not."

"Perfect." I beam at him, being nice like Ivy wanted.

I return to the fridge, rearranging it so that everything goes in correctly this time, feeling much lighter and in control. The turkey goes on the bottom. Smaller containers sit on top. Pie on the top level.

Except, the second, whole pie is missing.

I scan the counter, even though I could have sworn I placed it right under the microwave. Then I hear it—humming.

He. Did. Not.

I turn around, and there Grant is. Leaning against the wall, fork in one hand and abducted pie in the other. He raises a triumphant brow while shoveling the last bite.

I shake my head. "Are you serious right now?"

"What's wrong?" he asks breezily.

I'm so annoyed, all I can do is point an accusing finger at the pie.

Grant cocks his head to the side, eyebrows knotted like he doesn't understand what the big deal is. "I'm sorry, did you want some of this?"

"You know I didn't," I all but growl.

This is what he does. Every time I try to shove him out of my space, be it with subtle hints, cold shoulders, or outright actions, Grant just pushes back harder. Like showing up at mine and Ivy's birthday dinner, slipping in just long enough to crack a few of his jokes and make sure I felt the weight of his heavy stare. Or tonight, stealing an entire pie and inhaling it in record time, knowing it's not something I can ignore.

I may have chosen to guard my heart and shut the door on whatever we could have had, but he's been determined to make sure I can't forget him or the connection we shared. He's determined that I not have even a moment of peace when he's around.

Oh, but according to Ivy, he's the least petty person she knows.

"You've had a lot on your plate today," Grant says while his brown eyes taunt me. "Figured I could take care of one thing for you."

At that, he pushes himself off the wall, humming as he gets within striking distance. He tosses the empty pan in the trash and dirty fork in the sink.

"I'll get out of your way so you can finish up in here." His grin lingers as he disappears back into the living room.

Chapter Three

On a typical Matthews Thanksgiving, we eat dinner, eat pie, then officially start the Christmas season with a movie.

This Thanksgiving, however, is far from typical. Without Dad or Ivy, any inclinations I would've had for celebrating are gone.

So, I spend the next three hours cleaning every surface of the kitchen from the windows to the walls. I wipe baseboards, vacuum the living room, fluff couch pillows. Anything to keep my worry for Ivy and the babies at bay.

In the middle of wiping down the wood banister, the Pie Thief comes slinking out of the guestroom. He's in his jeans from earlier, but he's discarded his black sweater, leaving only a white undershirt.

The way it hugs his shoulders and biceps would be almost scandalous if it weren't so enticing.

His eyebrows jump when he spots me. "You're still cleaning? It's almost nine."

"Still cleaning," I answer with a dismissive air.

If I act like he's not here, or that I'm not still salty over the pie, he might just go back into the room.

No such luck.

Grant has himself a seat on the newly fluffed couch and turns the T.V. on.

I huff out a breath and get to polishing like my name is Cinderella, until a familiar saxophone melody reaches me. I turn back and find Grant has put on a movie.

"Why are you watching this?" I ask, automatically getting annoyed.

"Earlier Ivy told me y'all were planning to watch *Best Man Holiday*. Figured we could watch it while we wait to hear about the delivery," he says before propping his big feet on my daddy's coffee table.

I clutch my dust rag and polish spray and march to the couch.

Grant looks up at me with a growing smile that freezes when he notices my pointed glare. Then, he wisely sets his feet on the ground.

Before I walk away, he tilts his head, nodding at the spot next to him.

I shake my head emphatically. "I can't sit at a time like this. I've got way too much nervous energy." I search the room for something—anything—else I can clean to keep my hands busy. "Pass me that remote caddy. It needs to be polished."

"Polish the remote caddy?" He shakes his head. "Would you listen to yourself? Eve, I know you're worried about your sister, but I think you might be losing it. I'm gonna need you to put the Orange Glo down and relax."

My nose scrunches up at how Grant's trying to act like he knows how I'm feeling.

Only, anyone who even marginally knows me knows how protective I can get over my sister, and that I'm likely to run myself into exhaustion if I don't hear from her. Grant, admittedly, is more than aware.

"It's a movie, Eve," he cajoles.

It's not just a movie. It's him. Sitting there like he owns the couch, like he doesn't know he sets all my senses on high alert. Like I'm not one heartbeat away from crawling out of my skin. He expects me to sit next to him and pretend I'm not worried sick about Ivy, or that my pulse doesn't jump every time he looks at me, or that I'm not two seconds away from polishing the paint right off the banister just to stay busy.

Whew.

Okay, that's dramatic. Maybe I do need to take it easy.

Slowly and deliberately, I set the cleaning spray and rag down on the table. Without looking at Grant, I lower myself onto the far end of the couch.

Grant lets out an amused huff and turns the up volume.

"So, what, is this some kind of sequel?" he asks.

"Sequel? It's the third in the installment," I answer, and immediately regret acknowledging him. Now I've opened a door, and instead of enjoying the movie, he peppers me with questions throughout the entire first act.

"You mean he slept with his best friend's girl in college? And that man still lets him into his home?"

"It was a whole thing, and yes it's complicated, but as you can see they're trying to be adults about it. They're brothers."

"Brothers? Nahhhh. I'm telling you right now, if my brother ever pulled that kind of shi—"

"Hush! You're ruining the movie. If you want the why's and how's, stream the movies on your own time."

As unserious as Grant is, his running commentary does serve as a welcome distraction until the events of the day—and likely all of the pie he ate—catches up to him. One minute he's going off about unnecessary secrets, and the next he's fast asleep.

I turn the T.V. up loud enough to drown out his snoring so I don't miss the joke I've seen play out at least a dozen times. This time, however, I don't laugh. It's not the same without Dad and Ivy here to watch it with me.

I miss Dad's quips about friendships having run their course or how he would have tried convincing Ivy and me that Morris Chestnut's attractiveness is overhyped. Like somehow women from different generations, socioeconomic backgrounds, and cultures have all gotten it wrong.

I miss being the last one to succumb to the post-Thanksgiving meal coma as Dad inevitably fell asleep on his recliner, plate of crumbs perched precariously on the armrest, while Ivy tried hiding under the blanket to cover her own drooping eyes.

With Ivy on my mind, I reach for my phone to see if any text messages have snuck in, but there are none. I put it back down and rub a hand over my face.

How long could it possibly take for her to deliver two babies and call to let me know they're all safe and healthy?

A snore rattles from my left, and I look at Grant again. Grant who's sleeping like a newborn baby. I consider picking up the pillow separating my side from his and chucking it at his head. Why should he be able to relax when I can't?

I've got the pillow in my hand, ready strike, but hesitate. I usually only take small glances, but tonight I let my eyes linger as I really take Grant in. Strong jaw, broad nose, relaxed lips too soft for how much trouble they cause me. The rising panic fades, replaced with the usual mixed-up cocktail of grief, attraction, and warning settling heavy in my stomach.

This man, I think. Before the thought can go any further, my phone buzzes against the coffee table.

I lurch for it as my heart skyrockets. There's a text from Linda.

Nia and Amani have entered the world. Nia arrived at 12:32 am. Amani at 12:43.

My heart swells so much it hurts as the names of my sweet nieces are etched onto it. *Nia and Amani.*

We knew the twins were girls, but Ivy and Braxton had kept their names a surprise.

I love them so much and suddenly, I want to do all the things—order a plethora of giant bows and tiny bonnets, learn to sew and make them monogrammed quilts. Call up Dad and celebrate him being a first-time grandpa, then tease him over still being the only male on our side.

The last thought it enough to wipe the smile off my face as pain blooms in my chest, knowing that's the one thing I can't do.

Still, I want to share this moment with someone. I guess tonight that someone will have to be Grant.

I let the pillow fly, and it lands right against his face with a satisfying *thwunk*.

"What the?" He jerks awake, looking around before finding the pillow in his lap and glaring at me. "What was that for? I was just resting my eyes."

I roll my eyes to avoid admiring how handsome he looks all confused and aggravated. "You rested your eyes so well you missed the second half of the movie." I point to the rolling credits. "Anway, check your phone. We've got some good news!"

I sing the last part, and his sleepy annoyance instantly melts away. He digs out his phone and swipes it open. With the light from his screen illuminating his face, I see the exact moment his full lips curve into a smile.

Then, he's off the couch, pumping his fist like his team just won a championship. "Let's go!"

I'm not about to be out-celebrated, so I hop up too. "Let's go!" I shout. "I'm an auntie!"

I tip my head back, letting relief and excitement wash over me in an intoxicating rush. Grant must feel the same, because he grabs my free hand. He twirls me in a circle before throwing up a hand for a high-five.

I slap his palm, then we do the same but with our elbows, and finally we turn to the side and bump hips.

Only, Grant's so much taller than me, I have to hop to make contact.

When it's over, we're both laughing and breathless.

"Hey, you still go it," Grant says.

"Of course."

As if I'd forget our victory dance from game nights at Ivy and Braxton's. We won so many rounds of Pictionary, I could do the moves in my sleep.

My phone buzzes in my hand, breaking the spell of old, fun memories. I look away from Grant to see another text from Linda.

We've just received word that Ivy is all sutured up. We haven't seen her or the babies yet.

I frown at the message and read it again. "Sutured? Why would she need sutures?"

"Sounds like she had a c-section," Grant says. "That's typical for delivering twins."

I know it's typical, but that doesn't stop the panic from creeping back up.

"But why wouldn't they tell us she was going into major surgery to begin with? How is Ivy doing now? How are the babies? Do you think your mom has more information she isn't sharing?"

"Eve—"

I begin pacing in front of the coffee table. "I knew I should have been there. I'm her big sister and the only family she has left."

I should be there to watch over Ivy and make sure the medical team is doing all they can. What if something slips through the cracks and Ivy ends up like the mom she and I never got to know?

As my thoughts spiral, a tug on my arms brings me back to the present.

"Hey," Grant says, angling his head down to look at me. His hold is firm but not too tight, long fingers wrapped around and grounding me. "It's all good. I promise. My mom will let us know when there's more info. She won't keep you in the dark about anything. Okay?"

He stubbornly waits for my assent, relaxing only once I nod.

"Good. Now, this is excellent news. You're an aunt. We should be celebrating. Break out the wine." He smirks. "Ya boy could go for more pie. I'll even save some for you this time."

I let out a slow breath. "How can you have an appetite at a time like this?"

His eyes take on a serious edge. "Eve, look. There's one thing I don't play about—sweet potato pie. I haven't met anyone who comes close to making them like Grandma Simmons used to. Until now."

For as much grief as the pies were to bake, if Grant is to be believed, I *did* that. And as his serious expression morphs into a charming grin, I consider saying yes to the pie and more. Like the ghost of Christmas mischief is whispering in my ear that if I give into the urge to throw myself in his arms, everything will be okay. My sister, my nieces, my heart.

I draw my arm back, blocking out that dangerous voice. I've learned from my mistakes. Love isn't for me, and prolonged time with Grant spells bad news for my control.

I take a small step back so Grant's hands fall off while shaking my head. "All of the excitement is finally catching up with me. I think I'll just go lay down and try to get some sleep until we get another update."

I dare to meet his eyes, pretending like I don't see the disappointment he tries to hide, and walk away before I can do something I'll only end up regretting later.

Chapter Four

Despite what I told Grant, and despite it being close to midnight, I'm not tired in the least.

I sit on my old Queen-size bed worried about Ivy and once again wishing I would have gone to the hospital with her. I can't shake the feeling she needs me. She's got her husband and in-laws, but my intuition tells me it's not enough. She needs her sister there, too.

I'm going to send Linda a text just to make sure there aren't any new developments she hasn't told me about.

Right as I pick up my phone it starts vibrating in my hand with an incoming call from Braxton.

I immediately swipe to answer it. "Braxton, how is everything? Is Ivy okay? How are Nia and Amani?"

"Hey, Eve," he says, followed by a long exhale. "Sorry I'm calling so late. It was too much to type out."

"Too much to type? Why? What happened?"

I'm already off the bed and looking around the room for my keys and purse.

"We're okay, or, *will* be okay," Braxton says carefully. "I just need you to listen and not react, okay?"

"Okay."

God, where are my keys?

"Ivy is sleeping off the effects of the drugs, but otherwise she's fine. Nia and Amani..." My heart breaks at the sound of Braxton's voice cracking before he clears his throat and continues. "They came so early that their lungs haven't fully developed, so they have to be transferred to a Level four NICU."

I don't hear anything Braxton says after that, but I do finally find my keys inside my purse. Now I need to find my shoes.

This don't make no sense, I think, hustling from one side of the bed to the other. I had my shoes on all day, and now when I need to go somewhere they've up and disappeared off the face of the earth.

I fling the closet open and find a pair of flip flops with rhinestones I haven't worn since college. I put them on anyway and get a glimpse of myself in the mirror hanging on the door. To put it mildly, I look a hot mess.

"Eve, are you there?" Braxton's voice breaks through the fog.

"I'm here," I answer, turning away from the mirror. Who cares about fashion when you need to be there for your sister? "Which hospital did you say they're transferring y'all to again?"

Braxton lets out another sigh. "Methodist Hospital in San Antonio. But look. Eve, I need you to listen... You can't come."

His words knock the wind out of me and my hand freezes before I can turn the doorknob.

"What?" I ask, hoping I didn't hear him correctly.

"I'm sorry. There's just already a lot going on here with the transfer and Ivy has to wait for her doctor to give the okay before she can be moved. They said the visitor restrictions are even more stringent there, and they gave me all these damn papers with all this information like I'm supposed to know what it all means." I hear the shuffle of papers and edge of desperation in Braxton's voice.

Putting myself in Braxton's shoes, I realize how stressful the day has been for him. First it was running around the house to get everything ready for dinner. Then it was rushing to the hospital. Now it's getting the babies transferred. It would be a trying day for anyone, let alone a first-time dad.

And if it's been stressful for him, it's been absolutely crushing for Ivy. Which is why I need to be there.

"But I can help," I insist as my voice quivers.

"You can," Braxton says gently before his next words break my heart. "At the house."

I shake my head, already knowing what he's about to ask me.

Ivy and Braxton decided to move into our childhood home when they found out Ivy was pregnant. Only, it took so long to get the move approved by Braxton's job that they didn't get here until she was six months along.

I'd planned to take off all of December to help prepare the nursery and go through Dad's and my old things to clear the house and make room for their growing family.

Now Braxton is asking me to do it alone. Without him or Ivy. Without Dad. I know none of it can be helped, but this isn't what I'd planned for at all.

"Braxton..." I begin.

"It would take so much stress off of us if we knew Nia and Amani had their room ready for when we get home. And you won't even have to do it alone. Grant will help you."

He wants me to spend more time with Grant? With my heart and sanity intact?

For a second, I consider faking bad reception, pretending that the call dropped, and racing to the hospital anyway. But the thought of Ivy coming back home, exhausted and with even less time on her hands, keeps me from bolting. If I can't be by her side, the least I can do is make sure she has everything her and the babies need when she comes home.

"Eve, please," Braxton says, his voice breaking again.

I let out a long breath and set my purse down on the desk. "You know it's not even a question. Of course I'll do this. We're family. I just need you to promise to keep me updated. I want to know everything that happens."

"I will." Relief softens his voice, like a boulder's been lifted from his shoulders. "Thank you, sis. I know you'd rather be with Ivy, but I want you to know how much I appreciate this."

Braxton runs through the logistics of everything that needs to be tackled while I'm here.

"I know," I tell him when he repeats, 'The diapers are in the closet,' for the third time.

He's obviously running on empty, and I need him to rest if he's going to take care of my family.

"Don't forget, it was already in the plan for me to work on the nursery," I tell him. "You know I was all up in there, scoping the room out, as soon as I got here."

"And don't *you* forget, you're not alone. Grant will help too."

I withhold a sigh.

With how crazy this year has been, neither Ivy nor Braxton have had the opportunity to question how Grant and I went from partnering up at their weekly game nights, to me avoiding him at the wedding reception and every get together after.

"I don't know what's going on with you two," Ivy had said when I arrived two days ago. "And frankly at this moment, I'm too tired to care. I just need you to be a big girl and be nice while he's here. No rude remarks, no mean looks, and no sarcastic comments about the kitchen table being too small to accommodate him. He's my family and more importantly, he's nice. So promise me you'll be nice."

I committed to what Ivy asked, but I can't get myself to do the same for Braxton. After how easily I caved to Grant's smile, I have to draw the line somewhere.

"Can I ask you for one more thing?" Braxton says.

"Of course."

"Pray for a miracle. Ivy didn't want to bring this up to anyone and would probably kill me if she knew I was telling you this, but these eight months have been brutal on her without your dad. She's devastated he's not around to meet the girls. I know he always made Christmas special for y'all, and I'd hate if her first Christmas without him was spent in a hospital. Pray that Nia and Amani get strong enough for us to make it home soon."

A lump burns my throat. I press a hand to my chest, swallowing hard before I can answer. "I will," I whisper, and we hang up.

I kick my flip flops off and lay on the bed, staring up at the ceiling until it blurs.

Ivy and Braxton need a nursery for the babies, and so I'll give them one fit for royalty. Cribs on each side of the room with their beautiful names painted in gold. Changing tables in each corner and Ivy's rocking chair in the middle, right in front of the window where the light spills in. A room full of peace, warmth, and love. And I'll give them a house they can build their family's foundation on.

The image of the finished nursery is clear in my mind, but I'm questioning if this is right. Because staying here and playing house, as much as it's needed, while my twin is so far and out of reach feels very much wrong.

What would you do, Dad? How would you turn this disaster around?

That was one of his specialties—turning whatever mess life gave us into a celebration.

Like the time I offered to make dinner while he took care of the Christmas tree he'd brought home. I accidentally mixed-up bake for broil and burned the chicken to a crisp. Smoke came flooding from the oven, detectors were going off like it was the end of the world, and Ivy doubled over in laughter at my so-called cooking skills. Just chaos. Then Dad swooped in with a fire extinguisher, grilled up some hot dogs, and served them picnic-style by the newly lit tree. The scent of fresh pine covered my charred disaster, and somehow the night felt magical.

If Dad were here, he'd assure me that it's okay if I'm not at the hospital, and that Ivy and the babies will be fine. Then, he'd set about turning this place into a winter won-derland so not only would they have a beautiful nursery, but they'd also have a beautiful first Christmas.

And just like that, I know what to do.

I won't stop at the nursery and a few donation boxes. I'll decorate the house. I'll hang the lights, bake the cookies, and decorate the grandest tree this house has ever seen. Dad may not be here, but when Ivy walks through the door with her babies, she'll feel his love in every corner of the home he built for us.

I close my eyes, the weight in my chest easing just enough to let sleep pull me under as my Christmas plan finally comes together.

Chapter Five

"This don't make no sense," I mutter, flipping the wannabe slat of wood in my hands.

While sitting on the floor of the unfinished nursery, I scan for any indication that this is the L piece. L. The manufacturer couldn't label the pieces with stickers or even helpful numbers. Nooo, they had to go with letters in the faintest color of gray, which is almost impossible for these twenty-eight-year-old eyes to spot.

I drop the board onto the carpet and ball my fist before I'm tempted to throw it against the wall.

I am a family lawyer who's handled paternity cases messier than the likes Maury Povich has ever seen, navigated ex-spouses with storylines juicier than The Bold And The Beautiful, and set up custody schedules that could pass for NASA launch protocols. None of that, apparently, qualifies me to assemble a crib.

"Morning," Grant's deep voice sounds from the doorway.

I brace myself before slowly turning around to find him looking deliciously rumpled while watching me through half-lidded eyes.

"What are you doing?" he asks.

I pick up the instructions packet to give me something to look at other than him, squinting at the diagram. "I'm putting together the first crib. I told Braxton I'd have the nursery ready by the time they got home."

Grant folds his arms across his broad chest and lifts a brow. "That's funny. When I spoke to him last night, he asked for the *both* of us to do it."

I wave my hand. "Don't worry. I've got it handled. I figured with everyone gone, you'd want to head home anyway."

Grant shakes his head while pushing off the doorframe and turning to walk away, but not before I hear him say "I knew you were going to do this."

I chew on my bottom lip and look after him for a moment then turn back to the crib. I'm not claiming the guilt trying to work its way into my chest at his absence. The moment between Grant and me from last night, when I was emotional and therefore vulnerable to his charm, is over. I'm fully in control with a renewed purpose and plans.

"Aha!" I exclaim when I spot the piece I was looking for.

Twenty minutes later, I'm in the zone, finally making progress on the crib when the enticing scent of chocolate hits me. I immediately perk up, then wish I hadn't when I spot Grant freshly showered and groomed, strolling back in with a steaming mug. I hold in my gasp at the sight of marshmallows spilling over the top. He made my favorite—hot cocoa.

Which he keeps close to his chest as he walks right on past me.

"Hey, you don't have to do that," I say sharply when he sets his mug on the windowsill like he owns the place and begins opening the other boxed up crib.

No answer. Is this man really going to ignore me?

"I said I'll take care of the nursery. You can go back home."

Picking the mug back up, he finally meets my glare. "I heard what you said. I'm good over here."

His head tips back as he takes a healthy sip.

How dare he.

How dare he stroll on in here like I'm invisible. How dare he try to insert himself where he's not wanted nor needed.

He sets the drink back down with a satisfied "Ahh," then wipes the corners of his full lips.

Seriously, how dare he not even offer me a taste. That is, not offer to make me a cup. That's *my* dad's mug he's using after all.

I watch Grant for another five seconds as he rips into the box and pulls the materials out like it's so easy. *Puh-lease.* If I had muscles like that, I could Hulk out on the box too.

Teeth gritted, I turn around. If Grant wants to set up one of the cribs, *fine.* I won't waste my breath arguing. Besides, the sooner he finishes the sooner he can leave.

Pointedly ignoring the man behind me, I assess my work. It looks... okay. I just need to make it so that all of the slats lay flat instead of awkwardly on their sides. Yeah, I'm sure that'll make it look better.

Even though Grant messed up my flow, I get back to work, resolved to act like he's not here. Grant, however, makes it impossible. Every thirty seconds I hear a *slurp*.

Slurp.

Slurp.

Slurp.

By the twenty-third time, I'm ready to hurl a wood slat his way. I don't even understand how he still has any hot chocolate left. Is the cup bottomless? Did he walk in with a secret stash he's using to refill it?

I whip around, ready to rail into him, then snap my mouth shut.

His crib is complete.

It's only been like forty-five minutes. The manual says it takes an hour. I'm at ninety minutes and counting and still adjusting slats, so how did he finish so fast?

Grant pauses from breaking down his discarded cardboard to look at me and my struggle crib. He must read the promise of death in my glare because he wisely goes back to what he was doing.

It takes me another thirty minutes, but I finally take a step back and look at my work with a smile on my face, relief in my heart, and exhaustion I can feel down to my bones. I really should have gotten more than a few hours of sleep last night.

"Done with these two," Grant says casually.

When I turn around this time, he's dusting his jeans off while proudly looking at the *two* changing tables he managed to put together.

I square my shoulders and lift my chin. "Let's put one there," I say, pointing to the right corner. "And the other by this crib."

"Actually, I was thinking we should probably put one down in the living room."

I blink. "Why would we do that? It'll ruin the symmetry."

"Because it'll make their lives easier?" he says like it's obvious. "If they're downstairs with the twins, they won't have to come all the way up to change them."

He's got a point, but I hate that him making sense is ruining my vision for a beautiful, double nursery. Maybe it's the lack of sleep making me cranky or that I'm cocoa-deprived or that I've spent the last two hours in this room smelling Grant and being aware every time he's breathed, but I need him gone. For real this time.

"Look Grant, I appreciate your help, but I've got this. I can finish up the nursery for my nieces without your help. Besides, I'm sure you've got a lot that you could be doing back at your own home. In San Antonio."

Grant lifts a brow. "In case you've forgotten, they're my nieces too."

I take a step towards him. "Well, this is my house."

He crosses that invisible middle line that had been keeping us separated and scowls down at me. "Wrong. This isn't your house anymore. It's Braxton's and I have every right to be here."

"I don't need your help."

"It doesn't matter. You've got it anyway."

Even though I'm average height for a woman, my dad used to say the way I carry myself makes me seem bigger. Grant may tower over me but I make my spine as straight as possible so it feels like we're eye to eye.

Eye to eye means, however, that we're standing so close, I feel the warmth of his body heat and the small puffs of air as he breathes against my forehead. I smell the chocolate lingering on his lips.

That's all we do—breathe and stare until the air crackles with electricity that makes me feel dizzy and reckless.

And then Grant's eyes dip to my mouth.

I can't help but wonder, if he bent and kissed me right now, would it be one of those slow, exploratory kisses we shared at the wedding? Where I'd been desperate for his connection yet still wounded from Eddie and afraid it wasn't enough, that I wasn't enough? Or would we kiss like we've practiced a thousand times already? There's only one way to find out.

What am I doing?

I take a step back. It's not nearly enough distance, but hurling myself against the wall to get away from him would be a bit of an overreaction.

"Look, Eve," he says, his voice steady and firm. "I know you haven't been comfortable around me since..."

My whole body starts to lock up at where I think he's going with this.

"...everything," he finishes. "But I'm not doing this anymore. I'm not going to just stay away from *my* family because it makes *you* comfortable. I care about my nieces, and Braxton, and Ivy just as much as you do."

At his pause, I wonder if he'll say he cares about me. Is it foolish to actually *want* to hear him say it?

"I want to be here for my family," he says quietly, though the steel in his voice is unmistakable.

I inhale slowly. I could tell him that they aren't simply family—they're all I have left. Grant has another sibling. Grant has both parents. I only have Ivy. Now Ivy and Nia and Amani. And while this may not be my house anymore, it's the one thing I can keep from falling apart.

The unyielding earnestness in his eyes, however, keeps me from revealing my stingy, desperate thoughts.

"So, Eve," Grant says, inching toward me again. "I don't care if your plans include rearranging furniture in the whole house, cleaning the gutters outside, or watching a marathon of Christmas movies, I want in. I'm done letting you push me out of the picture just because it's easier for you." All I can do is blink up at him as he takes another step forward so that we're mere inches away. "I'm here Eve, and I'm not going anywhere."

He stares at me like he's daring me to deny it. To deny him.

For once, I don't know how.

Chapter Six

The dryer buzzer goes off, but instead of heading straight for the laundry room, I grab the paper I've been scribbling on all afternoon.

My mind hasn't stopped replaying Grant's words. *I'm done letting you push me out.*

As if he can just bulldoze his way into my life more than he already has and I'm just going to sing Christmas carols and take it. No sir. If he's staying, then I'm putting him to work.

Slam!

Grant's fork clatters to the table as I slap the paper down, pie crumbs landing on his shirt and his eyes going wild like he's under attack.

"Woman, what are you doing?"

"I'm showing you my plan." I plant my hands on my hips and raise an eyebrow. "Since you're determined to stick around, you can help me get the house ready for Ivy and the babies."

"And Braxton."

"And Braxton."

He leans back, eyes narrowed with suspicion. "A plan, huh? This feels like a trap. What, are you going to ask me to get something from outside in the middle of the night in nothing but my Christmas boxers, then lock me out?"

My brain short-circuits, picturing Grant in tight boxers covered in Rudolph heads with glowing red noses. Is that what he sleeps in?

I shake my head to get rid of the image. "Don't be ridiculous. It's a simple list. But if you find it too daunting, don't feel obligated to stick around."

Grant picks up the paper, studying my words like they're evidence in a courtroom. "Bake cookies twice?"

I cross my arms. "I've never made these cookies before. It was always Dad and Ivy, so I need to do a practice batch...or three, to make sure mine come out perfect." Grant already knows the kitchen and me don't get along, but my cheeks still burn explaining the why of it. "You know what? Don't judge my methods."

"Trust, I'm judging," he says before singing, "*She's making a list, checking it twice...*"

I resist the urge to snatch the paper back. The list is organized into three phases: baby prep, house prep, and Christmas prep. It's thorough and maybe even a little on the ambitious side, but I need to make sure we don't miss a thing.

Going by Grant's narrowed his eyes, it might be too extensive for him to handle. And if it is, good. He can go home and leave me to it.

"I'm pretty sure this list is just your way of bossing me around," Grant grumbles.

"Hey, you know I run a tight ship."

"Of that, I am aware." He laughs low and easy, and something flutters in my chest. I used to roll my eyes at that laugh, the way he seemed content with his laid back, go with the flow routine. Staying out late, sleeping in. I always wondered how someone who seemed to thrive on little planning and structure could be a successful basketball player turned financial advisor.

Grant's never been like Eddie, who appeared disciplined, always turning in early, especially when he was out of town, claiming he needed rest for work.

Of course, I turned out to be wrong about Eddie.

The dryer buzzes again and I march to the laundry room, eager to shake both the memory of Eddie and the warmth from Grant's laugh still prickling my cheeks.

Grant follows, munching on another bite of pie. "So, Your Honor, what's first on your grand plan?"

I decide not to comment on the old nickname he uses. He knows full well I'm no judge but thinks it's a funny way to call me bossy.

"Laundry," I say, then begin transferring clothes from the dryer to the basket.

When it's full, Grant shoves his plate at me and grabs the basket before I can. We move to the living room and station up at the couch, Grant on one side, me on the other, and the basket of clothes on the ground between us. I'm too far from the trash so Grant's plate goes on the coffee table. Then we get started.

When I grab a onesie, Grant follows suit, and for a while we fall into an easy rhythm, folding the small clothes into even smaller rectangles. I blindly reach down and my hand lands on a pink sock that's so tiny it doesn't even span the palm of my hand.

"It's hard to imagine anyone being this small," I say and Grant hums in agreement.

I find the sock's sister and fold them over each other before reaching for a white long-sleeved onesie. Before folding it, I bring it to my nose and inhale. It smells light and soft, making me think of bunny fur and warm kisses.

I'm so happy Ivy has the family she always wanted, but I can't help that persistent ache in my heart while folding clothes for her babies instead of my own.

I stayed with Eddie for too long. Wasted so much time on someone who wasn't all about me. And now, I wonder if I'll ever have the life I dreamed.

I fold the onesie, tucking the sleeves back then folding it in half until it takes on the same square shape as the one before and place it beside me.

I look over to Grant's side to see how he's coming along and pause when I find him looking at me. I can't fully read the expression on his face, but his eyes have grown soft in a way that makes my heart constrict.

"What?" I ask defensively when he doesn't look away. Those eyes of his see too much, and it's a battle not to physically hide.

"I just... nothing." He trails off and places the terry cloth robe he'd been folding down.

I wait a few more seconds, giving him room to finish what he was going to say. But he doesn't so I go back to my clothes, aware of every movement I make and watching Grant from the corner of my eye.

So I got a little sentimental over some baby clothes. God forbid a girl mourn the life she thought she was going to have.

"Did you see the packet of hangers anywhere?" Grant asks.

"Hangers? I'm pretty sure I saw some in the closet."

"I'll be right back."

He gets up and goes to the nursery upstairs and a minute later I hear his footsteps coming back down the steps.

"We can use these for their dresses," he says while holding the hangers out. Like everything else, they're small and appear even more so in his big hands.

"Of course," I say, wondering why I didn't think of that. It's such a simple, no-brainer idea, and yet Grant had to be the one to point it out. "Where did you pick up all this knowledge about babies? You're supposed to be the guy who knows about running plays and numbers on and off the court. Now you're talking about changing table locations and folding swaddle blankets like a pro. That's the kind of stuff you learn when you are an actual parent." I pause. "Wait—do you have kids?"

Is Grant somebody's daddy? He was only in the NBA a few years before rupturing his ACL and retiring, but who knows what he got up to during that time. We never discussed his love life during game nights.

One side of his mouth curves and he shakes his head like he's aware of my thoughts and suspicions. "No, I don't have any kids." He places a purple dress with an overlay of glitter tulle on a hanger then looks at me from the corner of his eye. "At least not any that I know of."

"You are so unserious."

He chuckles. "No, but really. No kids. Destiny came to live with me when she broke up with Todd. She was six months pregnant, so I helped her with pretty much everything for a while."

Destiny, Grant and Braxton's baby sister. She lives out of state so the only time I met her was at Ivy and Braxton's wedding. I remember her hair full of curls, her infectious laugh, and her adorable toddler.

"You've got first-hand experience with newborns because of your sister, and not because you're hiding away any kids," I tease. "I'll file that under 'Things I Never Knew About Grant.'"

"There's a lot you don't know about me," he shoots back.

That playful grin is gone, and he watches me expectantly, inviting me to ask more questions. I know there's more depth to him than simply being the easy-going guy who cracks jokes and lives to get under my skin, but I also know feeding into my curiosity would put me on a slippery slope. In just the past couple of days we've spent together, the jumble of emotions I normally get around him has faded, the attraction ramped up. But what if I get too close, misjudge his easy laughs like I misjudged Eddie's virtue, and end up the worse for it?

With effort, I shrug before tearing my gaze from his and focusing on the clothes in my lap.

Grant sighs. "Aiden."

I shoot him a quizzical look. "Excuse me?"

"Since you won't ask about me, even though I know you're dying to know, I'll tell you more about my family. My nephew's name is Aiden and he's four. He likes Legos and always beats me in Nerf gun fights. I keep my phone stacked with the latest games because Little Man shakes me down for it every time I come around."

My lips twitch at the thought of big ol' Grant having to surrender his phone to someone who doesn't even rich his hip.

"I'm sure the games you download for him are strictly for educational purposes," I say. Clearly, he's not going to stop talking so I may as well indulge him.

His eyes flash with a pleasure that makes me feel warm all over. "Of course. Nothing but the best."

"How often do you get to see him? They live in North Carolina, right? Or was it Florida?"

"Florida. And not as often as I'd like. Maybe once or twice a year now. That's where I was on Halloween, in case you were wondering."

"I wasn't, but thanks for the info."

"Uh huh, sure," he murmurs, unconvinced.

Fine, I did wonder why he hadn't tried making an impromptu visit while we were running birth plan drills. Grant's the kind of guy who'd unabashedly knock on the door and show up with something ridiculous like a red clown wig and shiny grill. Or a scandalous firefighter costume.

"And this is where you share something about your-self," Grant says, breaking the silence.

"What? Why?" I ask, startled coming out of my ridiculous fantasy. My mind is running too wild.

"Because I want to know more about you."

I slowly fold the pajamas in my lap, trying to keep my movements casual. "You already know about me."

"I know about the woman who's merciless at Uno but can't play Spades to save her life. I know about the woman who always brought a store-bought cheese board to each game night because she usually came straight from a meeting with clients."

"Charcuterie board. And trust me, bringing that instead of subjecting y'all to my cooking was an act of kindness."

His eyes dance, but he doesn't let up. "I want to know more."

His voice is smooth like velvet and my cheeks heat, pulse races. Not Grant making me all flustered.

I force a laugh. "I'm not that interesting."

"Try me," he challenges.

I roll my eyes. One thing Grant will do is keep pushing no matter how much I try to hedge him.

"Like your nephew, I also like building Legos," I say, feeding him an obscure but safe fact while adding the pajamas to my pile. "Remember those Legos we made for the wedding? They were my idea."

From the corner of my eye I see Grant nod slow and carefully, like I said something weird...*oh*. Of course he'd remember the Legos and subsequent kiss I laid on him.

Even more flustered, I shove my hand into the basket for more clothes, and grab something warm... which just happens to be Grant's hand.

Milliseconds feel like hours as I look down at our hands. My smaller one holding his larger one; almond brown mixed with honey. A quiet spark humming beneath our skin.

His thumb shifts slightly, like he's tempted to hold on, but I pull away.

"Sorry about that," I say, willing my pulse to calm way down.

"Why? I'm not."

My cheeks burn. I grab the nearest onesie and fold it with jerky motions, pretending his words didn't just curl through me like smoke.

"You know," Grant says after a long moment, "I used to think I'd have this by now."

I glance up cautiously. "Have what?"

"A family. A few kids." His holds my gaze. "A wife making me pies every day."

"Do not even," I laugh, but the intimacy of our hands touching has me breathless.

"I didn't say what kind of pie. Shoot, I'd take some of those microwavable chicken pot pies. My girl Marie Callender can throw down." He tilts his mouth into a grin then he leans forward, resting his elbows on his knees with his arm brushing mine. "It would just be nice to have someone to share it with."

His closeness is dizzying. His scent, warm and faintly spiced, wraps around me. I don't see him shift, but now his leg presses against me too and he doesn't bother to move away.

Neither do I.

It's that slippery slope again, and I'm heedless to the warning signs. Maybe if Grant would simply keep with the jokes and pie stealing it would be easy to push him away. But I saw the real yearning in his eyes at his admission. And now that he's opened himself up, the least I can do is reciprocate by giving him something real.

"I thought I'd have it all too," I admit, my voice soft. "I loved my little life here with Dad and Ivy, and always wanted a family of my own."

"You still can, you know."

I stare at the onesie in my lap, my fingers curling tight in the fabric. Grant's nearness makes it too easy to imagine. His hand on mine again. His arm around me. A future with no fear where I get to keep him. No more losses.

I can't. I can't let myself drown like that.

I fold the onesie with sharp precision and shove it into the basket. Then I stand quickly, putting distance between us.

"No," I say, not looking at him. "It's too late."

The feel of his leg pressed against mine lingers long after I race upstairs, wondering how he keeps slipping under my defenses and how to get it to stop.

Chapter Seven

I hate to leave plans unfinished, but I need an emotional break.

Braxton called this morning and gave me a little peace of mind with news that Ivy is already up and walking and the babies are settled into the new hospital. It wasn't much peace of mind—they are still away from home and me—but hearing the news was like catching the first few notes of "All I Want for Christmas Is You" drifting through the air on a hot August day and realizing the best time of year, along with cooler temperatures, is right around the corner. Plus, after folding Nia and Amani's clothes had me fighting back tears, I knew I needed to hold on to that newfound hope.

So, I'm switching gears and turning to Christmas Prep. Specifically, cookie baking. I've got my favorite apron on, have lined the counters with the ingredients for Dad and

Ivy's famous shortbread cookies, *and* I'm alone. Grant's in his room hopping on some "very important" meetings so I get to bake cookies without the pressure of his gaze following my every move.

I hum "Deck the Halls" while studying the recipe card filled out in Dad's neat script. After years of enjoying the benefits of him and Ivy making these, it's daunting to be the one measuring the flour, cutting the butter, and trying to make these cookies look like hearts instead of lopsided snowmen. But I press on, reminding myself this is only a practice batch. When I master them and Ivy is home to eat them, it'll be like Dad's right here with us.

When the cookies are as close to perfection as I can make them, I dust flour off my apron and slide the pan into the oven.

Minutes later the timer dings, I pull them out—and my shoulders sink. Instead of the neat little hearts filled with jam that went in, out comes one giant, brittle cookie with jam bleeding intermittently like a horror-filled Christmas crime scene.

I stifle a groan.

"Something in here smells good," Grant says, hand rubbing across his stomach as he rounds the corner.

He stops when we sees the pan.

After a moment his eyes flick to mine, then back to the pan, and a twitch plays across his lips. "What happened?"

"What do you think happened? I tried making cookies and got this lump instead." His lips tremble from holding in his laughter and I cross my arms, shaking my head.

"Grant, I am being so serious right now when I say your life is in mortal danger."

He holds his hands up in surrender but still approaches. He breaks off a piece, blowing briefly before popping it in his mouth. I cringe when he bites down. Shortbread cookies should not be that crunchy straight from the oven.

"Not bad," Grant says after a hard swallow. "Flavor's there. Style too." His gaze dips to my frilly pink apron. "I like the lace on you."

I swat his hand away when he runs a finger along the trim. "The flavor doesn't matter if the cookies barely come out edible." I yank the apron off before Grant can touch it again and toss it on the counter before groaning. "Oh, God. I'll have to run to the store for more ingredients." I throw my head in my hands for good measure.

"Okay, what's wrong with that? It's only a few minutes away, and it's not like we're in 2008 dealing with Black Friday shoppers."

I shake my head. "You don't know the half of it."

"If you're really scared, I'll be your bodyguard."

"Ain't nobody scared," I scoff, though I actually am. It gets scary trying to buy baked goods when everyone is in full Christmas baking mode. "And you wouldn't understand because you're not from here."

"Yeah, yeah. Don't worry, Big Daddy Grant will make sure no harm comes to Her Honor," he says, wrapping an arm around my shoulders like he's protecting me from an angry hoard.

His body is warm and hard, and perfect for snuggling against.

I immediately push him away.

Grant laughs, unfazed. "Seriously, I'll come. I need to grab a few things anyway."

"What things?"

"Groceries, what else? Unless you were planning to survive on turkey and hot chocolate?"

If it meant having peace without Grant around to push my buttons at every turn, yes, I absolutely would survive on turkey and hot chocolate as long as I could. But going off Grant's challenging stare, I know he's going to find a way to come shopping with me anyway. Besides, he'll wish soon enough he'd just stayed here.

I roll my eyes. "Fine, but I'm driving."

"Fine, but *I'm* picking the music," he says, smirking on his way past me to grab his coat.

Grant's tune changes real quick when we get to the store and arrive at the baking aisle.

"What...what happened?" he asks, horrified.

It's pure chaos. It looks like we've entered a scene from a post-apocalyptic movie. Shelves emptied out, flour coating the floor, a package of sugar laid out in the middle, torn in half as if people were fighting over it and they both lost.

"Oh all this?" I say, injecting an air of nonchalance while secretly laughing at Grant's stunned expression. "People around here treat their Christmas baking like an Olympic sport. There are always so many cookie exchanges and bake-offs starting as soon as Thanksgiving is over. You're lucky we didn't have to come out here on Black Friday."

"It gets worse than this?"

"Let's just put it this way: witnessing a grown man get trampled over some confections is one of my core memories."

I wheel our cart forward, but Grant latches onto my elbow. "Wait. I don't think we should go down there."

"Don't be ridiculous—"

"Out of my way!"

Grant and I both jump to the side when someone comes barreling by us. It's an older man with a Santa hat on top of his head and a manic look in his eye scanning where the flour should be.

He shouts, "Hallelujah!" before reaching way, way back into the shelf and emerging with a gold-labeled bag that he holds up high like he's on top of Pride Rock.

Grant and I both gasp when the man's head swivels in our direction, giving us the stink-eye and daring us to try rolling up on him and his flour. As if we'd ever be foolish enough. When he finally drops the bag into his basket and clears the aisle, Grant lets out a low breath from behind me.

I smirk at him over my shoulder. "Remind me. Who's supposed to be guarding who?"

Leaving Grant there sputtering, I make my way to the same shelf the man found his treasure. There's one lone store-brand bag of flour left. After a glance to the left and then right—just in case someone tries to roll up on *me*—I reach for it with a small thrill of victory. The second I step back though, my heel slips on the coated floor, sending me airborne.

Before I can hit the ground, warm hands catch me around the waist, and I'm pulled against a solid chest.

"I got you." Grant's voice is low and so close to my ear.

I swear, no matter how much I fight it, these little moments keep happening between us—like fate is trying to push us together.

Fate grabs my chin. Fate jerks my face up toward Grant. Fate punches through my chest, squeezes my heart until it forgets how to beat when our eyes lock. And fate anchors my feet to the ground, keeping me right in his arms even though I know I should move away.

Someone behind us pointedly clears their throat and Grant stiffens, tugging me even closer, ready to throw down in defense of me and my flour.

"Eve is that you?" a familiar voice asks.

I gasp and lurch from Grant's arms so fast that my heel slips. Again. Before I hit the floor, Grant catches me. Again.

"Really?" he mutters, steadying me.

Once I'm upright, I shoo Grant's hands away then look up and find Ms. Thomas watching the whole spectacle with wide, amused eyes.

Ms. Thomas has lived across the street since before Ivy and I were born and was the only adult on the block who could tell us apart. She was always so sweet, opening her yard for the neighborhood kids to run wild during the summer and spoiling us with her gingerbread cookies during the holidays. When Ivy and I moved away for college, Dad would tell us about her stopping by with containers full of pork chops, catfish, or her homemade tamales, and I would tell him to snatch her up so he could keep eating good.

She was a great friend to him and took his passing hard.

"It is you!" Ms. Thomas says, stepping away from her basket with her arms outstretched.

Grant grunts as I shove the flour at him and brace myself for Ms. Thomas's hug. She's eighty percent signature faux fur coat, twenty percent sweet grandma, and one hundred percent love.

We exchange hellos and I tell Ms. Thomas how I'm in town to help Ivy. All the while, her gaze volleys between Grant and me. Subtle at first, until she just full-on stares at him while talking to me.

"And who might this tall glass of mulled wine be?" she asks.

I don't even bother looking at Grant as he lets out a deep chuckle, knowing he's eating this up.

Ms. Thomas sends me an anything-but-subtle nod. "Well done, Eve. He's *much* more of an upgrade from your ex."

"You can say that again," Grant mutters in a similar, anything-but-subtle manner.

"Actually," I cut in. "This is Grant. He's Braxton's brother, so Ivy's brother-in-law. He's helping me at the house." I add quickly, "We're not together."

Ms. Thomas squints one eye like she doesn't believe me before her gaze drops to the flour Grant's holding. "So...are you two baking?"

"I'm the one baking," I tell her. A light bulb goes off, and I remember the years' old cookie exchange between her and Dad. "And don't worry, I'll make sure to bring you your Christmas Eve dozen this year. It'll be the same shortbread cookies Dad and Ivy always made."

Her smile freezes while her eyes tell it all. "Okay, sweetie. You... do that."

Her living across the street has meant she's been witness to the smokey aftermath of my many failed baking and cooking attempts. But God bless her, she's never turned down a lopsided cake or burnt casserole, though I'm pretty sure her tastebuds have suffered.

"Well, I'll let you two get on with your shopping," she says.

She scans the flour section, her lips tugging down at the now entirely empty shelves. Then her gaze slides to the bag Grant's holding.

Now I'm not one to tussle, especially physically and outside of the court room, but I *will* throw down if it means making Ivy and Dad's cookies. Christmas won't be perfect for her without them.

Grant casually slides the flour behind his back. "Well, it was nice meeting you, ma'am," he says, all polite Southern charm. "And don't worry, I'll make sure Eve here doesn't forget your cookies."

Looks like I don't need to worry about Ms. Thomas coming for the flour. Grant's clearly recognized her true feelings about my kitchen skills and decided to weaponize it. I'd be insulted if it wasn't so effective.

Ms. Thomas startles, then recovers with a strained smile. "Thank you. How wonderful of you."

She snatches a bottle of molasses and scurries off faster than I've ever seen her move, though I'm pretty sure I hear her mutter, "Eve is making shortbread. Lord have mercy."

As she turns the corner, I elbow Grant in his side at his snicker, hiding a smile of my own.

Chapter Eight

Two hours later we're back in the kitchen surrounded by grocery bags. They cover every counter space plus the kitchen table.

"Hey, what's all that moanin' and groanin' for?" Grant asks as he finds room for the last bag.

I lean against the sink and let my shoulders fall. "Moaning and groaning? I am exhausted. How is getting groceries with you somehow worse than Ivy dragging me to Ulta all 21 of their 21 Days of Beauty? And who is supposed to eat all this food?"

Grant shakes his head and calls me a *lightweight* before tugging me away toward the table.

"Hey!" I say in protest, but quiet down as he steers me to a chair.

"Rest up, Princess. You still got some baking to do."

I shake my head. "Nope. Not today. The butter has to be at room temperature, and thanks to *someone* trying to buy out the whole store, it won't be soft for at least another hour. I fear I'll be too tired by then when I need to be alert for baking. I don't have forever to nail these before Ivy gets back, and they need to come out perfect."

He twists his lips to the side, considering. "Did you soften the butter earlier?"

"Yes."

"And did the cookies come out perfect?"

Grant's lucky looks can't kill. I give him my best death glare anyway. "I swear, it's like every day you wake up and choose trouble."

"Consider me guilty as charged," he says before looking me up and down, slow and appreciative. "Good thing I know a smart and sexy lawyer who can get me off the hook."

Straight to jail! I want to shout, but then he'll know that heated look and smooth baritone is getting to me.

"I don't know why I even bother with you." I grab my phone from my pocket so I have something else to focus on.

I do my best to ignore Grant as he rattles around the kitchen finding space for all the food, opening cabinets, and turning on the microwave. After a few minutes, though, it feels wrong sitting here while he works. I don't know if that's guilt talking, or because I'm not used to a man actually pulling his weight without having to be asked.

Just when I think I should offer to at least put up the three boxes of cereal Grant couldn't choose between, he suddenly appears, his big form looming over me.

"Bam!" He drops a wrapped stick of butter in front of me the same way I did the list, and it lands with a plop.

"Bruh, what are you doing?" I ask, clutching my phone to my chest. If I have to use it as a weapon, I will.

"You said you need your butter at room temperature. So, there you go." He folds his arms across his chest looking all proud and smug. "Don't say Big Daddy Grant never did anything nice for you."

"This is the second time in one day that you've referred to yourself as Big Daddy, and I need you to get that under control real quick."

I quirk an eyebrow, staring at Grant expectantly until he bows in defeat. "Yes, Your Honor."

My lips twitch and I turn back to the butter before he can see the smile threatening to break through. I press a finger against the wrapper, and it gives. Perfectly softened.

I stare up at Grant. "What kind of holiday sorcery is this?"

"No sorcery. All Big Dad—" he catches himself. "That's all me."

I get up and follow him back to the counter. "If you're trying to tell me you're a handy man, baby expert, *and* kitchen genius, I will send you packing right now," I say lightly but I'm only halfway joking. No man is this perfect at everything.

"See, I told you there's a lot you don't know about me." He slips the apron over my head, then twirls a finger for me to turn around. His voice comes warm at my back as he ties the strings. "But for your information, my mom taught me that trick. One time she forgot she was supposed to bring cookies to my league's end of season party happening that day. She showed me how to heat a glass dish to get the butter ready in a flash."

When he's done, I face him again. "Let me guess, she only forgot because *you* forgot to tell her you signed her up?"

He presses a finger to his mouth. "Shhh. As far as she's concerned, it slipped her mind in the chaos of three kids and five different activities."

I know I'm in trouble, because the way his lips curve around that finger make mine ache, and I'm imagining him bending down to lay the same touch against my mouth.

"Alright," Grant says, thankfully oblivious to the scene playing in my mind. "Let's get this cookie party started. What's first?"

"You're staying?"

"Someone's gotta make sure you don't let Ivy or Ms. Thomas down."

And of course he doesn't give me the chance to argue. He slips on one of Dad's old aprons and waits for me by the hand mixer and bowls he already set up. I grab the butter off the table, and we get started.

Grant watches me cream the butter and sugar, then takes over when it's time to add the eggs. His hands may be made for basketballs, but he cracks the delicate eggs with careful precision, allowing only the yolks to slide into the bowl.

"What?" he asks when he catches me staring.

My cheeks heat and I shake my head. "Nothing. You're just so zoned in. It reminds me of how Grant got Ivy and me tickets to one of your games when they first started dating. It was your turn to make some free-throw shots and while the crowd was going wild, you were focused on nothing but the goal post."

He pauses for a beat, and I catch the flicker of sadness in his eyes before he covers it with mock seriousness, shaking his head. "Basketball does not have goal posts. Totally different sport. And of course I'm in the zone. There's one thing I don't play about—egg cracking."

Ivy mentioned before how Grant doesn't like to talk about basketball, and now I see it for myself. His old career is clearly an open wound for him, and I have no intention of poking it.

So, instead I squint at him and tilt my head. "Wait a minute, didn't you say the same thing about sweet potato pie?"

A one-shouldered shrug. "There's two things I don't play about."

"Okay, Dr. Eggman. Let's move on to the flour."

He fills the measuring cup with an even layer of flour.

"Just dump a little at a time," I tell him while holding the hand mixer at low speed.

But my little and his little aren't the same, because the next second a cloud of flour explodes between us. I squeal as it covers my sweater, my face, and no doubt my hair.

Grant laughs while fanning the air.

"You did that on purpose!" I accuse.

"I promise you I didn't," he claims, while his laughter suggests otherwise.

He grabs a dish towel off the counter and steps closer, swiping gently at my cheek.

His hand lingers longer than necessary but he pulls back. "See? All better."

I turn back to the bowl to finish the dough, willing my heart to calm down.

We shape the dough, add jam to the centers, and this time Grant suggests to let the cookies chill in the freezer so they'll hold their shape. Another trick his mom taught him.

When we pull the first batch out of the oven, I gasp. "They're beautiful."

There are actual, individual cookies—not a blob.

"So, these are the famous Matthews cookies, huh?" Grant says beside me.

I nod with my smile on full display. They look so good. Exactly as they should.

"Yeah. Ivy and Dad used to make these every Christmas."

"Just them? Why not you too?"

"I never had the knack for baking, which I'm sure you've picked up by now. There's a reason Ms. Thomas looked like she wanted to book a vacation to the Bahamas to be far away from my cookies." I giggle remembering her reaction. "Dad and I used to collect snow globes though. There's this huge Christmas market the town has, and we'd go every year and pick one out together. It was our little father-daughter tradition."

"A Christmas market you say? You taking me this year?"

I roll my eyes. I hadn't given the market much thought, and now my heart immediately says no. It won't be the same without Dad.

"I don't think I'll have the time. There's already so much more we have to do around here before everyone gets home. We need it to be—"

"Perfect," Grant finishes. "As you've said." He grabs two cookies, heedless of their too-hot temperature, and puts them on a small plate he then sets aside. "But it is Christmas. You're spending all this time doing things for everyone else and worrying about what they need to be happy. What about what you need, Eve?"

What I need is to fill the Dad-shaped hole in my chest. I need Ivy, Nia, and Amani here. My heart won't be full without them.

Yet Grant eyes me, looking like a man ready to provide all of my needs.

"Let's do a taste test," I say quickly.

Grant grabs the cookies and tries to shove one in my mouth like a groom feeding his bride. I give him a flat look, grabbing his wrist with one hand and taking the cookie from him with the other. When I bite into it, my eyes roll back.

"Oh, my God," I say, stuffing the rest into my mouth. Warm, buttery sweetness perfection.

Grant pops his into his mouth and begins nodding while pointing at the rest of the batch. "Oh yeah. You did this."

"We did it," I correct him. Because without his help, I would have been battling dough blobs.

"I guess Ms. Thomas will be happy she stayed home after all," I say, smiling up at him.

Grant's eyes rake me over, laughter lighting them. "You still have flour on your cheek."

"What? Please don't tell me I've been standing here talking to you this whole time looking a mess." I swipe at my face. "Did I get it?"

"Not even close. Here, let me."

He reaches up to brush my cheek, the pad of his thumb both warm and a little rough. The smell of cookies clings to his skin, sweet like the smile he aims down at me.

After three strokes I'm sure he's got the flour off, but this time his hand doesn't move away. Neither do his eyes. They're intense and sure, and as the air between us thickens all I can think is that this man keeps surprising me.

He's knowledgeable, helpful, funny. Attractive.

Too attractive.

His eyes dip to my mouth and before I can stop myself, I wet my lips. His jaw sets with quiet determination as he leans in, and even though I should step back, I tilt my head up.

As the space between us narrows, his hand moves to cup my face. Our breaths mingle, mouths centimeters apart.

Ring!

Back to life. Back to reality.

"Ivy's calling," I say breathless, immediately recognizing the ringtone.

"Give me a break," Grant utters quietly enough for me to act like I don't hear.

My pulse races and my knees wobble like Bambi on ice as I scramble to the table where I see Ivy wants to video chat. The phone doesn't want to stay in my jittery hands as I fumble to pick it up, but I manage to get a solid grip and swipe to answer as I bolt from the kitchen. Away from Grant and what could have been a kiss I'm not sure I'd recover from.

Chapter Nine

Whew, Lord. Saved by the ringtone.

I don't slow down until I'm safely in my room, with a door, stairs, and kitchen to separate me from Grant.

"Hey Twinnie," Ivy says once her picture pops up.

"Ivy!" I cry, fighting back emotion.

The whiplash from getting swept up in Grant to seeing my sister after so much worrying is nearly enough to bring on a wave of tears.

"Are you okay? What's wrong?" she asks.

I step away from the door while shaking my head. "Nothing's wrong. You caught me finishing something up in the kitchen and I ran upstairs."

Ivy hesitates. "Is... the kitchen still standing?"

"Hardie-har-har." I let out a dry laugh. "Don't worry, the kitchen remains intact."

She wipes invisible sweat from her forehead, and I cut my eyes at her while also inspecting her as much as I can through the screen. She rests against a gray headboard, so I know she's not at the hospital. Some of the pregnancy-induced swelling has dropped from her face, which I'm unsure is a normal part of being post-partum or a sign that she's losing weight too quickly. Lastly, her eyes have dark circles underneath, letting me know she isn't getting enough sleep.

"I'm so glad you called," I tell her, making my way around a box and to my bed. "Braxton's been keeping me up to date, but it's not the same as hearing from *you*. Are you getting enough rest? Eating? Do you need anything? I still have your in-laws' address saved in my Amazon from the gift I sent on their anniversary. Just say the word and I'll have whatever you need sent over."

Ivy closes her eyes in the middle of my rambling, but a faint smile spreads across her lips. "I'm fine." She pauses, reconsidering her words. "Well, I'm doing okay, given the circumstances. Yes, I'm eating. And no, I don't need you to send anything up here. I've got everything I need."

At least she doesn't try to lie and tell me she's been sleeping.

She opens her eyes and looks at me. "Braxton is doing a good job of taking care of me and the babies."

"And how are my beautiful nieces? I can't wait to meet them and love on them."

"They're fighting to get strong enough to come home. Braxton's mom and dad are at the hospital with them right now. I'm supposed to be sleeping but I can't," she admits. Her eyes water and she closes them before any tears can fall, taking a moment to compose herself. "My nurse says if I want my milk to come in then I need to take care of my body, but it's so hard."

I wish I could reach into the phone and pull her into a hug. "It'll come in Ivy, try not to stress about it. You know that will only make things harder."

"I know. It's just..." She takes in a shaky breath full of unleashed emotion. "None of this is what I pictured. I don't even care about the c-section or these big ass underwear they gave me that practically sit under my boobs. I just want to hold my babies all day without a timer or the sound of breathing machines in the background."

"Oh sissy, I'm so sorry you have to go through this. Just know everything you're feeling is natural," I tell her softly. It kills me that we have to do this over the phone instead of in person where I can be there for her to lean on. "This part is temporary. Nia and Amani will be out of there before you know it and you'll get all the time in the world with them."

"You can't know that," Ivy whispers.

"Nope. Don't go trying to flip the script on me. What was it you used to call me when there was something you weren't sure about and I was?"

Ivy sniffs and her lips twitch. "Know-It-Eve."

"That's right. Don't start acting brand new just because you had some babies. I *know* my nieces will get stronger. I *know* they'll be okay."

After a few moments of deliberation, I see the moment Ivy decides to trust in my word. She tilts her chin up and smiles at me, this one reaching her eyes.

"You're right. My babies are strong. They'll be okay."

"I know that's right!"

We smile over the screen, hope shared between us.

"So," she says after a few moments. "How is it going with you and Grant? Braxton and I have a bet as to how long it will take you to drive him out the house."

"What? You're betting on me? Why would you do that? You know that's bad twin juju." I dodge her question, not ready to tell her there is a lot going on—almost kisses, lingering touches, evolving feelings...

"Are you two at least getting along?"

"Yes?" Especially if getting along means wanting to strangle him one minute then kiss his pie coated lips the next. "And the nursery's almost finished."

Ivy lets out a yawn that sets one off in me too. "I can't wait to see it. Thanks again for doing this for us. I don't know what I would do without you."

"That's what big sisters are for."

She nods, looking good and tired. However, knowing her like I do, once we hang up, she won't easily give up and fall into the sleep her body desperately needs. She'll be back to worrying over Nia and Amani, when the best way she can take care of them is by taking care of herself. And while I might not be there in person to ensure she's doing just that, there is another way I can help.

I walk to my old bookcase I started clearing earlier and pick up a worn paperback. "Remember this?" I hold the book up to the phone.

Ivy squints at the screen. "Is that *Nutcracker and Mouse King*?"

"Yup. Remember how we used to make up our own adventures for them, imagining Marie with tiny afro puffs and the nutcracker with a gold chain?" We both laugh. "Are you still down to fight a freaking rodent to live happily ever after with someone who's greatest talent is cracking nuts?"

"Whoa, not too much on my man now," Ivy jokes while rubbing her eyes. "Look, Braxton's cool and all, but the nutcracker? Well, that's mine, and I'mma stick beside him."

I climb onto the bed and prop my phone on the pillow before opening the book.

"*For the entire twenty-fourth of December, the children of Medical Officer Stahlbaum were not permitted to step inside the intermediary room...*" I begin.

Ivy's quiet as a mouse as I read and just as I suspected, when I make it to the section titled "The Protégé" and glance at my phone, she's sleeping.

Chapter Ten

I t's the next morning. Time to get my plan back on track and continue the Baby Prep.

I wasn't simply giving Ivy lip service last night. I *know* my nieces will get strong and they'll all be home for Christmas, so the house needs to be ready.

I march down the stairs ready to babyproof. I'm armed with a box full of outlet covers, bookshelf anchors, cabinet locks, and corner guards, as well as a glare I'm not afraid to use if Grant tries getting too close.

No more side quests; no more flirting.

When I land in the living room, he's not there. Pausing in the hallway, I don't hear any humming or movement coming from his room or see him in the kitchen as I continue on.

The heavy box makes my shoulders sag—not the disappointment of thinking he's clearly left without telling me.

Really. It's relief. In fact, I hope he'll be gone all day and really give me some space. I can throw my pajamas back on and blast some Christmas jams while I'm working.

I set the box down just as the back door opens.

"Ah!" I scream as cold air blasts my back. Then, I turn and see Grant, looking all rugged with a scruffy jaw and long-sleeved henley that hugs the lines of his shoulders. My stomach drops, heat blossoms and turns into butter-flies. I am in trouble.

"Oh good, you're up," Grant says, and it could be my imagination, but I swear today his voice rings as silky as Stevie Wonder's to my ears.

I need to get a hold of myself.

"Can you come here?" he asks. "I need your help with something."

Before I can figure out what he's up to, he disappears back outside. I stare at the door for a few moments, wel-coming the building irritation. I've got things I'm trying to work on; I'm not at Grant's beck and call.

Still, I trudge to the shoe rack to put on some tennis shoes and grab my coat.

When I step out to the back yard, the slap of frigid air against my face makes me gasp. You never can tell what kind of weather you'll get in Central Texas as win-ter approaches. I can recall a few Christmases Ivy and I spent playing outside, in shorts, because the days were so warm. Even though it's cold now, I'm not holding my breath that it'll stay this way come a few weeks.

"Over here," Grant calls from the shed.

I see him kneeling beside the big green tubs full of decorations.

"What are you doing?" I ask, battling the wind to get to him as it whips my locs to and fro.

Grant looks up, unaffected by the wind though the tip of his nose has a slight red hue from the cold. "Did you realize that every house on this street already has their decorations up? Since this is the only one slackin', and since it's on your list, I figured we could knock it out today."

"Today? I was going to babyproof everything. Besides—" I turn my back against another gust of wind and raise my hood. "I'm not sure if we should be doing anything in this weather." Not to mention I don't want him to mess up any of Dad's old ornaments.

Grant smiles into another box. "Here's what I was looking for."

It takes me a few seconds to tear my eyes away from his handsome face made even more attractive by his excitement. When I finally see what he's holding up, I smile back.

"You found the lights!"

"Yes ma'am."

He takes the string of lights in both hands and extends them to study the bulbs. Red, yellow, blue, green—the colors of my childhood.

"Wait, are these—" Grant begins.

"Traditional incandescent lights. They were Dad's favorite. He absolutely refused to use anything else. Listen, one year, Ivy and I accidentally bought LEDs. I kid you not, Dad spent three hours stringing lights only to then turn them on and realize we got the wrong type. You'd think after all that work that he'd take it as a lesson to not let us shop next time but roll with it, right?" I look up at Grant who's watching me with an amused grin and shake my head. "Nope. Not my daddy. He took every single strand down. He returned them the next day and started over."

Grant lets out a low laugh. "That explains why there's at least twenty unopened boxes of these things in here then."

"There are not."

Grant quirks an eyebrow and gestures me to look inside the bin. I lean forward for a peek and giggle. Grant's right. Dad did stock up on the lights.

Grant laughs with me. "So, about putting them up now?" He holds the lights up.

I sigh, long and dramatic. I guess I can babyproof later. "Fine. Let's do it."

His answering grin is bright and genuine, and my stomach is back to doing somersaults. I can see Grant actually likes all this Christmas stuff. And I like that about him.

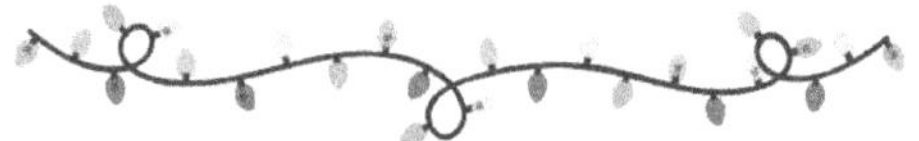

I'm going to take these lights down and strangle somebody with them. Grant by the looks of things so far.

"Come on, Eve," Grant drawls behind me. "No one's gonna care if the lights look more... artistic. From the curb it all shines the same. Besides, this isn't a competition with the neighbors."

I snap my head around and scowl. "Yes, it *is*. At least it always was to Dad." I yank the stupid strand straighter and try to force the bulbs to sit in a neat line around the pillar.

They still won't lay flat how I want, and I'm this close to giving up.

"You know," Grant says, slowly inching toward me. "I could always do it for you."

It's the third time he's offered since I've been working at this. First, I declined because I wanted to be the one to decorate it like Dad. Then I declined out of principle, not wanting to be undone by the lights. Now I see it's been a losing battle all along.

"Ugh. Fine," I huff and let the lights fall into Grant's waiting hands.

Of course, he fixes in two minutes what I've been battling for half an hour. His long arms loop the cord neatly and evenly, his motions quick and sure.

He steps back, admiring his work with a self-satisfied—bordering on smug—grin.

I narrow my eyes. "I could have done that if I had the wingspan of a pterodactyl. You basketball players and your long arms."

His eyes tighten slightly, and he picks up another bundle of lights. "I'll get these strung up on the roof."

Watching him walk away so abruptly is not a good feeling and I can't help but mentally kick myself for that little basketball comment. I hadn't meant to poke at his wound and know I should apologize. But he moves quickly and is already up the ladder, so I'll shelve that apology for later.

For now, one more pillar needs to be decorated and since I hurt my handyman's feelings, I'll have to do it myself. I hold in a silent sob and pick up another strand of lights.

When I'm done, my pillar looks noticeably different from Grant's, and not in a good way. I cast him a pitiful look, but my stomach immediately drops when I see that he's all the way on the roof, lying flat while attaching lights to the gutters below. Dad never did it that way. He always stuck to the ladder.

I don't know if what Grant is doing is safe, but I refrain from yelling out so I don't startle him.

"Lookin' good!" Ms. Thomas calls from across the street.

I turn to see her standing by her car in her fur coat and kitten heels, shooting us a thumbs up. I wave but before I can turn back to Grant, she calls out, "Eve dear, look at these!"

She holds some woven socks from a bag. "I got them from the Christmas Market. I'm about to turn on some hot chocolate and get nice and cozy."

That sounds delightful and makes me long to visit the market myself, though I know I won't.

I open my mouth to compliment Ms. Thomas on her style and activity of the evening when a strong gust of wind blows my hood back. Ms. Thomas's gaze darts toward the roof, and her eyes go wide.

I whip around just in time to see Grant roll, then drop like a sack of coal onto the yard.

"Grant!"

My heart seizes as I sprint to the side of the house. He's face up in the grass, eyes closed.

"Oh my God, are you okay?" I drop to my knees with my hands hovering helplessly above him as I scan for anything that could be broken. "I'm going to call the ambulance." My fingers scramble for my phone, but they're shaking so bad it slips and lands right on his chest.

"Ow," he groans.

"You're alive!" The surge of relief makes me dizzy.

His eyes slowly crack open, heavy with pain but locked on me.

"Don't scare me like that again," I tell him, my voice cracking. "How could you think going on a roof on a windy day was a good idea? Do you have any idea—"

His lips crash into mine.

For a heartbeat I freeze, too stunned to process that he's actually kissing me. But then his hand cups the back of my head, anchoring me to him, and I melt.

My eyes flutter shut and I kiss him back as all that control I've been clinging to slips right through my fingers.

My hand finds his cheek, stroking his skin. It's cool beneath my palm, but his lips are hot and soft and taste faintly of hot cocoa—of course this man made some without offering me any.

How dare he.

I lick his bottom lip, chasing every drop of sweetness, and am startled to realize it's not the cocoa that's sweet. It's him. And I am utterly lost in him. I don't care about the howling wind or the cold ground beneath my knees. This addictive kiss drowns out all else.

He squeezes the nape of my neck, fingers tugging my roots. I sigh into his mouth, willing to give him all that he asks in this moment.

"Honey, are you okay—oh!"

Ms. Thomas's voice brings everything to a screeching halt.

I gasp for air, looking for the good sense that left me the moment Grant's lips found mine.

"Well, I see everything is okay here," Ms. Thomas says, already scurrying away. "I'll just leave you two lovebirds to it."

I turn back to Grant. Although he fell back to the ground when I pulled away, his lips are curved into a blissful smile.

"Why did you do that?" I ask, proud of how steady my voice sounds given that I'm still reeling on the inside.

I kissed him! Again! Or, rather, he kissed me. But I kissed him back. Boy, did I kiss him back.

Grant shakes his head slowly as if coming out of a trance. "On the way down, I swore if I lived, I'd stop wasting chances. Then I opened my eyes and saw an angel hovering over me." His eyes clear and his mouth quirks. "Seemed like a dumb time to hesitate."

My cheeks burn hot. "Well, I'm no angel. I'll tell you that much. We'll chalk that little episode to head trauma."

I help pull him up, gripping his arms to make sure he's steady.

He winces and rolls his shoulders but seems otherwise unharmed. I can't say the same for my nerves. I don't know whether to yell at him more for climbing onto the roof, yell at him for kissing me, or pull him back down and make him do it again.

As usual, when it comes to Grant, my emotions are out of control.

"Gotta say…" Grant dusts grass from his pants while waiting for me to look at him.

I shake my head, already knowing that he's going to say the most ridiculous thing to make this whole situation even more complicated.

When I still don't look up, he tugs my hood back over my head and gently tips my chin with his finger until our eyes meet.

"The fall was worth the kiss," he says softly. "And judging by how you kissed me back, I'm not the only one who wanted or liked it."

Chapter Eleven

How is Grant going to try and tell me how I felt about the kiss?

Last I checked, he's not a mind reader nor body language expert. Him declaring something doesn't automatically make it true.

'I'm not the only one who wanted or liked it.'

And if I *did* like it? If I thought it somehow managed to top the kiss we shared at the wedding? If I've daydreamed of his warm hand caressing my neck, feeling the stubble of his mustache prick my lip, how he looked like a man who knew exactly what he wanted—so what?

I cannot fall for Grant.

One: he's Braxton's brother. I am not about to turn Ivy and me into those cliché twins who fall for a pair of brothers. Just... no. Two: I'm not in the market for another heart break. If Grant and I became a thing that ended in disaster, which seems to be the way of life for me, it would be a million times more awkward at family events. It's been impossible to keep Grant at a distance as it is. I'd have to do something drastic like lock him up in the shed to make sure I never saw him again.

"The light's green," Grant says beside me, snapping me out of my spiral. "Quit thinking about kissing me again and drive."

My foot slams the gas and the truck I'm driving lurches forward before stalling as I shift to First Gear. It happens two more times before the car behind us blares their horn.

"Well, happy holidays to you too," I grumble as they go around and speed past.

Out the corner of my eye, I see Grant grimace and rub his neck.

"You did not get whiplash from a little bit of rocking," I tell him, refusing to take his bait or talk about the kiss.

I get the truck moving and continue down to the Christmas tree farm.

It's been two days since the incident. In that time, I've organized baby supplies, sorted old household items into donation boxes, and rearranged the living room a handful of times. And Grant's been there every step of the way, doing all he can to ensure the kiss stays on my mind. So today I've decided I need some good, fresh air of the pine variety.

"I can't believe these are the best Christmas songs they can come up with," Grant huffs as a painfully slow version of "Sleigh Ride" drags on. "They could at least play something from this century."

"Just turn the radio off if you're going to have something to say about every song that comes on," I snap.

We had to use Dad's old Chevy since neither of us wanted to strap a tree to our cars, but that leaves us without a Bluetooth connection or even an aux cord. My patience is hanging by a thread with his constant teasing about the kiss. I don't need his complaining mixed in.

Grant does turn off the radio, then swivels toward me. "So, about that kiss—"

"I just remembered," I cut in quickly, my voice higher than normal. "There should be a case of CDs in the glove compartment."

Grant chuckles but reaches for the small handle. Crisis averted.

"I used to have some of these," he says, flipping through the selections. "You care if it's not Christmas music?"

"Nope. Whatever is fine by me."

I don't see what he picks, but a moment later Tamia's voice pours through the speakers.

Grant relaxes in his seat. "This era hits different, huh?" he remarks and starts singing along.

It's like he knows 90's RnB is my kryptonite.

I've always been a sucker for love songs. The kind that make you long for love when you don't have it, and appreciate it all the more when you do.

I didn't realize until now, but I stopped listening to music after Eddie.

The beat flows, the storytelling and soulful lyrics speaking to me now. They paint a picture of how life could be if I were brave enough to open my heart again. To have what Ivy and Braxton have. What Mom and Dad had. And as I glance down and see Grant's fingers tapping along to the beat against the seat, I long to reach over and grab on. He wouldn't let me down like Eddie did, right?

Grant catches me looking at him and I direct my gaze back to the road, just in time to not miss the entrance of Oh, Christmas Tree!

"Remember, we need something at least seven feet tall," I tell Grant after parking. "And the stronger the pine smell the better."

We get out and he makes it to the front of the truck before I do, holding his hand out. I pause, surprised he wants me to take it, until I realize he's gesturing me to go ahead of him. I stuff my hands into the pockets of my coat so I'm not tempted to reach out for his hand anyway.

I stop before we get to the entrance, right next to their makeshift hot chocolate stand where you can enjoy a warm treat while browsing for five dollars. The price seems a little steep to me considering it's served in a Styrofoam cup with no added marshmallows.

"Alright, why don't you take the left side, and I'll take the right," I say. "Now, they do have some of the best-looking trees, but be careful of who helps you. Some of these sales associates forget this is supposed to be the season of goodwill and start inflating prices like everyone's ballin'. Text me if you find something good."

Grant frowns. "You don't want to find one together?"

"There's so many trees here, it'll save time if we divide and conquer."

He hesitates but nods his agreement. I take off, speeding through the threshold and heading off on my side, determined to find peace and pretend the kiss and Grant's not-so-subtle reminders don't exist for a while.

I need to find the perfect tree. One Ivy will love.

With a deep inhale, the pine-scented air hits me sharp and sweet. When I came with Dad last year, it took us over an hour to find "the one." And then a new worker tried to overcharge us—big mistake. He didn't realize we'd been coming here for years, and that the one thing I hate most is people trying to get over on others. Especially at Christmas. Especially when the "others" are my family. I went full lawyer mode, and we walked out with a tree so discounted Dad said he finally knew how my clients feel when I win their cases.

I weave through the rows, relishing the soft spiky needles brushing my fingers, weighing each tree I pass. Some are that perfect dark green I'm seeking but don't reach my shoulder. Some have the height but gaps of branches that would be awkward to fill with ornaments.

When I get to the stand of mistletoe in the back my face heats and I back far away. The last thing I need is for Grant to pop up and get any ideas.

I keep going and pause in front of a tree that could work. It's shorter than I'd hoped for, but full and lush and would look wonderful wrapped in twinkling lights. I step back to get a better view and pick up Grant's voice.

"Excuse me, how much is this one?" he asks.

"For that height and density, you're lookin' at two hundred," the worker says and I frown.

Grant whistles while I try peeking through the trees to get a look at the worker.

"For that amount does it decorate itself?" Grant says under his breath.

"Sir?"

"Nothing." Grant sighs. "Do y'all trim the trunk?"

"Yup. It's an extra twenty-five dollars," the worker says.

Now I know he's lying, because ain't no way.

"What do you think of this one?" Grant asks me when I come stomping down the row.

I freeze in my tracks and gawk at the tree he's holding upright. It perfectly checks off all requirements: color, height, shape, and fullness. It looks like it came straight out of a magazine.

I beam at Grant. "I love it."

His chest puffs out.

Then, I let the smile slip right off as I turn to the employee.

I should've known.

The guy's face drains as his eyes go wide. Good, he remembers me too.

"We're interested in this tree," I say sweetly, "but did I hear right that it's two hundred dollars?"

If this guy is smart, he'll think very carefully about his response.

"This one?" His face scrunches up like he's got a tough deliberation going on in his mind, then nods, having come to some conclusion he missed that should have been obvious. "You know what? I must've gotten my trees mixed up. It's actually one-sixty."

Maybe I should be pleased, but I'm not. He's ready and willing to play nice with me, but where was that energy for Grant? He was happy to treat Grant like some big guy with deep pockets and no tree awareness.

I cross my arms. "Uh huh."

"*And*, we're throwing in an extra twenty percent off for couples," he offers.

"How very magnanimous of you, but we're not—"

"How much to trim the trunk again?" Grant interrupts.

"No charge, boss! You get it for free." The employee's eyes emphatically beg Grant to take the offer.

"Is this the tree you want?" Grant asks me, gently brushing my arm with his free hand. The touch is light and fleeting but sends a small shockwave through me.

I drag my gaze away from the worker to meet Grant's eyes. I'm mad that the employee tried to take advantage of him and don't want to give in, but it's exactly the kind of tree Dad would have picked. I know Ivy will love it.

When I nod, Grant winks before turning back to the worker. "Alright, we'll take it."

Fifteen minutes later we've got the tree loaded in the truck bed and are heading back home. The scent of pine fills the cab, blending with the sweetness of the cocoa Grant finagled—free of charge—before we left.

"What's that smirk for?" I ask Grant as we roll smoothly through an intersection framed with oak trees wrapped in white lights.

"It was nice having your scary scowl directed at some-one else for a change," he teases, eyes glinting with mis-chief.

"My scowl isn't scary," I grumble, even though we both know that's a lie. I've worked on my scowl throughout the years to intimidate opposing counsel and in general to be left alone.

Grant chuckles, a deep, warm sound that vibrates through the cab, but my stomach twists as I consider just how many times he's been on the receiving end of my scowls. Too many. And for all the wrong reasons.

The heater hums low, filling the silence that follows. Outside, passing storefronts glow with Christmas lights, but I can't enjoy the festive sight with the weight of guilt settling heavy on my shoulders.

Before we reach the next intersection, I swerve into the nearest parking lot, throw the truck in park, and take a steadying breath. "I owe you an apology."

"An apology for what?" Grant asks, his brow furrowing at the seatbelt's sudden tightness against his chest that keeps him from fully turning his body toward me.

"For how I've treated you," I say, though it's harder to squeeze the words out than I expected. "I know I haven't exactly been welcoming these past couple of years. I don't really know how to explain it, but every time I saw you, I was right back to the night you told me about Eddie cheating."

Grant doesn't interrupt. He just watches me, the fading sunlight softening his face. The seatbelt, however, stays tight across his chest, refusing to let him turn more than his head.

"And it's not like you did anything wrong. If we're being real, you saved me from a lifetime of regret. It's just…" I close my eyes as the emotions of that night crash back. My heart doesn't ache anymore, but I still remember the sting—Grant's voice, resolute as I denied what he was trying to tell me, the proof on his phone of Eddie's arm around another woman at a freakin' basketball game no less. A heavy breath escapes me. "I really thought I had everything figured out, you know? All my hopes and dreams were tied to a future with him and finding out he didn't feel the same was humiliating and devastating all at once. My life blew up, and then there you were, being all kind and gentle and funny, trying to make me smile when all I wanted to do was break down. My feelings were always just so jumbled around you, and then after Dad died"—my voice catches. "It was like the grief never stopped piling on."

I open my eyes to find Grant still straining to move against the seatbelt, though it's obvious he's trying to do so inconspicuously.

A soft laugh escapes me and I reach over. My fingers brush his arm as I unlatch the buckle. "There. These old trucks can be finicky."

He takes in a full breath and is finally able to face me fully. It's more intense, but he deserves to be able to look at the person apologizing to him.

"I know none of this excuses my behavior," I continue, "but I hope it explains it. I am sorry, Grant. And you were right the other day—it was easier to push you away. Not that you actually stayed away," I add in a weak attempt to lighten the mood.

Grant's face is unreadable until finally the corner of his mouth lifts in a slow smile. "Does that mean you're done trying to push me away?"

My mouth opens to respond, but nothing comes out. Am I done? It is exhausting fighting this pull I feel toward him.

He chuckles low and dangerously, knowing exactly how flustered he makes me. But of course, that's not enough for him. His hand finds mine, his fingers brushing over my knuckles before his thumb traces slow circles against my nails. The contact sends a shiver through me, steadying and undoing me all at once.

"Eve, I appreciate and accept your apology. Losing Eddie and your dad hit you hard, I get that. I'm sorry you were hurt by me telling you about Eddie, but I'm not sorry for telling you the truth. He was never good enough for you."

"Thank you."

"I remember what it was like when my world turned upside down."

I don't say anything, silently urging him to keep going.

"When I got drafted by the Spurs, I thought I had it all lined up to get fame, championships, a fat shoe deal." He pauses. "And a trophy wife."

"Oh my gosh, be so for real."

"I am being real! I told you I want a wife and kids. And, well, I want her to look good too."

I shake my head. Grant and his forever jokes.

As quickly as it comes though, his laughter fades and his face sobers. "Then I ruptured my Achilles. Physically, I recovered with surgeries and therapy. But realizing I'd never return to the level of performance and that my professional career was over..." His voice trails off. "It nearly broke me."

"How did you come back? How did you find yourself through the pain? I've managed to keep going, but it still feels like pieces of me are missing. I'm so afraid of losing anyone or anything else," I whisper.

Grant squeezes my hand. "It wasn't easy. I mean, basketball was life. It was all I cared about since high school. More than my family, as much as I hate to admit it. I missed birthdays, weddings, holidays, all while thinking that once I made it big, I'd take care of them and make up for lost time. Then when it all ended, I figured I didn't have the right to call them. Like I'd wasted my shot with them too."

"You could never, Grant. Your family loves you."

"I know." His voice drops, his pain raw and unfiltered. "But I didn't believe it then. I thought I had to push through on my own. It wasn't until my sister came to *me*, of all people, that I was able to look beyond what I'd lost and see what I still had. I realized I could still show up for everyone I cared about. That's why I'm here now," he adds. "For Braxton, Ivy, and the twins. For you."

Warmth spreads through me, filling every corner of my chest. I knew Grant was more than his jokes and easy charm, and here he is, proving that layer after layer resides a man determined to show up for his family. A man who never wanted to hurt me but cared enough to tell me the truth despite the pain. A man who refuses to let me push him away.

I take in a deep breath, feeling the shift in the air, the way it makes my stomach swirl with nerves and affection and something dangerously close to hope.

I let out a shaky laugh, carefully untangling my hand from his to get us back on the road. "Well, I'm glad you want to show up for me, but I'll tell you right now—I'm no trophy wife."

"Fine with me," he says, voice relaxed and warm. "As long as you make pie, I'll take you."

Heat crawls up my neck and I have to bite back the smile pulling at my lips. I keep my eyes fixed on every car, every traffic sign in the distance. Because if I look at him now, I'm certain Grant will see just how much I want to be taken.

Chapter Twelve

The sun has disappeared by the time Grant and I make it home. Christmas lights dominate the street, turning the block into a glimmering winter wonderland in hues of white, yellow, blue, and purple.

We wrestle the tree inside and set it up in the same rustic tin stand Dad picked out years ago. After trimming the branches to make it look more uniform, I scrunch my nose at all of the needles on the floor and wonder who's going to sweep them up. Grant on the other hand studies his sap-sticky fingers, apparently amused by how they cling together then snap apart.

When his eyes lift to mine, awareness of how ridiculous yet adorable he looks warms my chest, but there's a glint there I don't trust. And for good reason it turns out—he stretches his tacky hand to me, going for my face.

"Don't you dare!" I squeal, ducking under his arm.

He's big and fast, but my aversion to getting messy puts some extra pep in my step. I slip away as his other hand darts out, grazing the air where my cheek was.

"That's right boy," I taunt. "I float like a butterfly. Sting like a bee. You ain't gettin' any alley-oops on me!"

Grant looks utterly pained as he shakes his head. "You do know you mixed boxing and basketball metaphors, right? And that they don't go together?"

I shrug. A sport is a sport.

"How about this—stop chucking out bricks." Dad used to yell something to that effect at the T.V. It feels right.

Grant's frown makes my stomach tighten. Maybe I pushed too far after he opened up in the car about his old career.

Then he lunges.

This time I'm not quick enough. He catches me by the waist, one arm locked around my back, the other hovering near my face. Up close, I see in addition to sap, it's covered with lint and tree needles.

"Don't do it, Grant" I plead, poking my lower lip out. "Please."

"You shouldn't have talked all that trash," he says with mock menace, inching his hand closer.

Unable to bear the sight, I close my eyes tight. I'm at his mercy and accept my fate.

After a moment, his finger taps my nose then he stands me up.

I peek one eye open. "That's it?"

He smirks down at me. "Consider it a warning. But keep with the bad terminology, and you won't be so lucky next time."

As ridiculous as it is, I'm really starting to like that smirk of his. The way his eyes shine playfully and the corner of his mouth lifts.

That same mouth that was on mine two days ago, as Grant has been insistent on reminding me.

I let out a shaky laugh as awareness of how close we are, and how much I want him to kiss me again, hits all at once. The faint scent of pine still clings to him, and warmth radiates off his chest. After our heavy conversation in the car, it's a lot to take in.

I'm not trying to run away, but I need a breather.

I clear my throat and take a careful step back. "Well, you've made your point. And now I'm going to get cleaned up. Who knows what you put on my face."

He's still grinning as I head for the stairs. "Probably a good idea."

"If you know what's good for you, you'll do the same," I say, feeling unusually giddy as I look over my shoulder and catch Grant's eyes trailing after me.

After a quick shower, my mind is all over the place. I turn over each and every one of our interactions for the past two weeks. The more I think of letting our mutual attraction run its course, the more sense it makes. And somehow, *that* realization makes me panic. Wanting Grant shouldn't feel dangerous, but it does. Because wanting anything this much hasn't ended well before.

I tug on the holiday pajamas Ivy gifted me and grab my phone. I don't know what to do and need my twin to listen to me spiral, then assure me that whatever step I decide to take with Grant, I'll be fine.

But the call goes straight to voicemail. I set the phone down, trying to fight the tightness in my chest.

I hope her and the babies are alright. The tree is up, and the house is almost ready, but none of it will matter if they're not here come Christmas morning.

An unexpected knock at my door sets my pulse racing. Obviously, it can only be Grant, but this is the first time he's come to my room. What could he want?

I block out the taunting voice in my head insisting he's here to sweep me off my feet. That he felt the shift in the car just as much as I did and, being Grant, he's not about to let up now.

Also being Grant, he's probably here to ask if I'm fine with him finishing off the cookies.

But as I open the door, the first thing I note is how uncertain he looks standing in the hallway. Like he's as nervous coming to my room as I am having him here. Then, I laugh.

He's in the same red, green, and black pajamas as I am. And where my bonnet is black with a cheetah print band, he's got a green durag on.

"Let me guess," I say, trying to sound serious but a few giggles slip through. "Ivy had those waiting for you when you got here?"

"Yo, and here I thought I was special," he says, all the while his eyes sweep slowly from my head to fuzzy-sock-covered toes.

"Right. So, what can I help you with?"

He holds up a plate of our shortbread cookies. "Dessert? I didn't want to eat them alone."

"You mean, you need a co-conspirator for your week-long sugar binge?"

He shrugs but a quick glance at the ground lets me know he's not as confident as he's trying to appear. "Someone's gotta do it, and you're the only one here so..."

That crooked smile of his should not affect me the way it does. And yet, I step back and grant him entrance.

I get the weirdest sense of Déjà vu when he walks in. It feels like I'm in high school having a boy in my room for the first time. Dad's stern voice is in my mind, telling me to keep my door open, my bed empty, and my lips to myself.

"You can set the plate next to the lamp," I tell Grant when he stops beside a box full of old books.

Once he turns, I do a quick scan around my room to make sure there's nothing embarrassing out in the open. It's mostly packed up, aside from the old snow globes Dad and I picked together lined up on my dresser.

There's a snow globe featuring a snow woman with a wig and pink scarf. A city square with shopping bags piled under a tree. A father and daughter building a snowman. They vary in size and shape, some glass, some plastic, and each one holds a special place in my heart.

"What's this?" Grant asks.

I look to see what he's talking about then rush to his side and snatch an old notebook away.

"What is it? A diary?" he asks.

"No. It's a junk journal."

Which is so much more than a diary. It's an old notebook from high school full of drawings and ramblings, lyrics and pictures. Hopes and dreams from when I was young and bright-eyed.

Grant lifts an eyebrow. "That's like a scrapbook of sorts, right? Destiny had a few of those. They were always full of things like 'Boys Suck.'" He pauses then looks at me with eyes full of hope. "Can I see it? Please? I want to know what you were like when you were younger."

I inwardly groan.

I miss the Eve I was two weeks ago who would have kicked this man out of my room with nary a thought. Because this Eve I'm morphing into wants to let Grant into the deepest parts of her.

"Fine." I shove the book at him before I can change my mind. "But you better not laugh. If you do, I'll never show you anything ever again."

He wipes all traces of a smile. "Yes, Your Honor."

He sits on the bed and opens the journal, and I have to interlock my fingers so I don't snatch it right back up. I found it the other day, tucked behind some books I figured Ivy would never find with her nosey self. There's nothing too juicy in there; however, knowing how dramatic I was as a teen, I can't help but cringe as Grant's large fingers flit through the pages.

I let his chuckle slide when he comes across *my* huge ALL BOYS SUCK spread. His smile is still there when he finds a photo of Ivy and me giving the camera our best 'duck lips' pose. But when he finds the zoomed in drawing of a snow globe, his face shifts.

"Tell me about this one." He gently tugs on my hand, pulling me down beside him.

I swallow, looking at a pencil sketch of parents and their two kids standing in front of a modest house while snow flurries dance around. "It's the family I was supposed to have. And, well, you know how well that turned out." I tug at my hand but quickly give up when Grant makes it clear he doesn't want to let go. "It's not that good anyway. I'm pretty sure it was practice for an art entry I never ended up submitting."

"Why do you do that?"

I blink up at him. "Do what?"

"Try to make yourself smaller." His frown deepens. "You said you weren't good at baking, but you made that amazing pie and these bomb cookies I'm about to demolish. You talk down on your art like anyone off the street could have drawn it with as much detail and emotion. And even now, you've turned Christmas into some kind of project that's *just* for Ivy. You don't let yourself admit how much it means to you." His voice softens and eyes that see me too much don't let up. "When do you get to enjoy the holiday?"

"When Ivy and the babies are here to enjoy it with me," I answer automatically, though the words don't land as firmly as I mean them to.

The air between us grows heavy. I don't know what to think or say. I started this whole 'get the house ready for Ivy' because I want her and the babies to have the perfect home coming. Ivy has had an incredibly difficult year without Dad.

But, I lost Dad too. I've been clawing my way through the same grief. Maybe I deserve to stop and taste the cocoa instead of just stirring it the same way he would have. Maybe I need to let go of the guilt of not being by Ivy's side and let a little joy back into my own life.

My gaze drops to Grant's hand still wrapped around mine. Maybe that joy is within my reach, closer than I would have thought.

"Okay, time for your initiation," I say, needing to bring some lightness back.

"Initiation?"

"We're watching *The Best Man.* You had way too many questions during *Best Man Holiday*, so it's time to get you caught up. Knowing the lore is required for staying in the Matthews household."

"Don't you mean Matthews-Simmons household?" he teases, easily picking up where our playful mood left off, and for that I'm thankful.

"Yeah, yeah." I move to the edge of the bed, making room for Grant to get comfortable. "Grab the cookies."

As the movie plays, I can't help sneaking glances at Grant—cataloging his laughter at the jokes, the way he scoffs at the messy love triangle reveal, how he mutters, "Nah, he's wild for that," under his breath. The more he reacts, the more I find myself relaxing, and leaning into his warmth. So, when he wraps his arm around my shoulder, I let myself sink into him.

Grant was the last man who held me, and his embrace is just as comforting now as it was at the wedding. Better even.

I wrap an arm around his middle, snuggling in deeper and letting his scent wash over me. I'm surprised that the mix of soap and pine clinging to him smells even better than the Christmas tree itself.

"Thanks, you smell amazing too," he murmurs. "Like frosted berries and vanilla. All I've wanted is to stay close to you and breathe it in."

I realize I said that out loud, but my eyelids are too heavy for me to take it back or even be embarrassed.

I do, however, manage to tell him, "Don't let any crumbs spill on the sheets," before falling into a cozy sleep.

Chapter Thirteen

I wake up to warmth.

There's the flannel sheets and the sun weaving gold through the sheer curtains, yes. But there's also the heat of Grant.

His arm is hooked across my waist, his chest curved over my back, and I can feel his heartbeat thudding softly at my temple.

He must sense me stirring because his fingers begin to move in a lazy rhythm up and down my spine, like this is something we do every morning. I soak it up.

"Take me somewhere you love today, Eve," he murmurs, voice gravelly with sleep.

I turn just enough to meet his gaze, sleepy and serious. "What about everything on the list?" I ask.

"No lists today. Just you, showing the man you're obsessed with your favorite place."

I snort. "That's a stretch."

He chuckles. "Okay, okay. It doesn't have to be your favorite place."

"That's not what I meant, and you know it."

"No, I don't," he says, amused and so happy with his little jokes. "Now, somewhere that makes you smile."

I settle deeper into his hold. There's still work to be done around the house. I'm not done packing up our old things or finished with the nursery. But Grant wants to know what makes me happy. How can I not be touched?

A glimmer of light bounces across the snow globes on my dresser, catching my eye, and I smile.

"I know the perfect place."

I hold a candle out for Grant to smell.

He leans down, inhales deeply, and hums. "That smells like dessert."

"It's Snickerdoodle. Do you think Braxton will like it? He can put it in whatever room he'll use as his office."

Grant's look tells me all I need to know.

"Fine." I set the candle down with an apologetic smile to the vendor. Before we move on though, I grab and pay for the gray and navy scarf I saw Grant eyeing when we reached the booth.

"Eve," he says with exasperation.

When we came to the Christmas market he didn't want me paying for the parking, or the pictures we took with Santa, or the hot chocolate. I do like saving my money where I can, but I don't like a man trying to tell me how to live my life.

"It's too late. I already bought it," I tell a scowling Grant. "You might as well wear it and stop trying to act like you aren't happy."

I hold his cup of chocolate while he puts the scarf around his neck, and sure enough a crooked grin takes over as he runs his hands down the soft material. "How do I look? Good, huh? You don't have to say it, I already know."

Yes, he does look good. And no, I will not admit it out loud.

"Come on," I say, handing him his cup. "Let's keep walking. I need your help finding something for Braxton. I have no idea what to get him."

"First of all, this day was supposed to be about you. Second, once you're a parent, gifts don't matter as much. Get something for Nia and Amani. He'll survive."

"Uh, no. When I become a mom, I one-thousand-percent still expect my loved ones to splurge on me."

"So, it's *when* now, huh?"

I bite the insides of my cheeks to hide my smile. It's the holidays and I'm at my favorite place. I'm allowed to be optimistic about the future. That it has a little to do with the man walking beside me is just a coincidence.

"Besides, I already got Ivy something," I say. "I'll feel bad leaving Braxton out."

Grant drains his drink, tosses the empty cup into a passing bin, and threads our fingers together. "I'll help. But first, you're skating with me."

Why is Grant trying to act all strict today? Better question—why do I like it?

I follow his gaze to the rink at the center of the market. Families, couples, and even a few pros glide around with ease. When I meet Grant's challenging smirk, I know he's expecting me to push back and probably downplay having any kind of skating skills.

Well, he got the right one today.

"You've got a deal."

It doesn't take long to realize Grant is all bravado and no bite. While I glide onto the rink, he straddles the rubber edge like the ice is going to jump up and grab him.

"Come on," I coax.

He steps fully onto the ice and seems to completely forget how to work his limbs. His knees buckle and arms flap wildly before he catches the railing.

"Why did you suggest this if you can't skate?" I ask, skating backward in front of him.

"Because I saw that picture of you out on the rink," he admits, watching his feet like they're about to take off without him. "Figured this used to be your thing."

"You did this for me?"

He risks raising his eyes to meet mine. "How many times do I have to tell you today is about you?"

I'm filled with the urge to reach out and hug him, but I know that would only make him fall. So, I settle for a heartfelt, "Thank you, Grant."

He winks and it sends my pulse skyrocketing. "Any time."

And then he falls flat on his butt.

We're both laughing as I help him up.

"Look, I appreciate what you're doing here," I say, "but I want you to have fun too. We can walk around some more and get lunch. I saw a vendor with chicken and waffle kabobs. There's also roasted chestnuts if you're feeling more festive."

"How about you go skate while I work on getting the hang of this," he suggests.

"Are you sure?"

Grant nods and makes a shooing motion before grabbing onto the railing again.

I hesitate, but the ice is calling to me. "Okay. I'll only be gone for a little while. And oh, here's a tip: keep your legs slightly bent as you move forward. If it feels like you're going to fall, lean forward so you fall on your hands. The last thing we need is for you to end up in the hospital with a broken tailbone."

"Yes, Your Honor."

And I'm off.

My intent is to only skate around the rink three times then help Grant off.

On the first loop, I revel in the cool air against my face and the way my blades slice through the ice.

"Looking *goodt!*" Grant calls when I pass him by.

I go around again, easily navigating around groups and couples, picking up speed and remembering how it feels to fly. I used to spend whole afternoons doing this. Maybe I should again.

When I loop back, Grant is being escorted around by two little girls. He bends his knees, hunches his back to match their height, letting them lead him across the rink with all the patience and amusement in the world. The sight steals my breath.

I picture him with his nephew, knowing he'd be a fun uncle with his jokes and penchant for games. With kids of his own, gently leading and pushing them to achieve their dreams.

I picture him with...me. Waking me up to gentle caresses and sweet kisses. Inviting Braxton and Ivy to game nights at our house. Coming up with more silly victory dances after demolishing them in Pictionary.

"My Lord," I whisper, my heart beating wildly.

It's too much, too fast. Three weeks ago, I was actively avoiding the guy, now I'm daydreaming of morning caresses?

I force my mind to slow down and stay here, in the present where I've got ice in front of me.

I lift a leg to test my balance. For a few seconds, I skate on one foot without so much as a wobble and smile. I've still got it.

I spot Grant back by himself across the skating rink. He leans against the railing, watching me with a soft smile that makes all my insides warm. I show him my skills, switching to the other leg, doing a little spin, then a curtsey. He claps in the best show of encouragement before promptly sliding down the wall and landing on his butt. Poor guy.

When I reach him, he holds out a hand. "Just how good were you back in the day?"

"You're looking at the two-time Winter Wonderland Invitational champion," I say, slipping my hand in his.

We skate side by side, painfully slow but together.

"You know," he says softly. "This place is like that snow globe you drew. Different setting, but same feeling. Cozy but still full of life. I see why you love it here."

"I used to spend whole days here. Shopping, eating, skating. There's nothing like it." I bump his arm and immediately grab him when he wobbles. "Sorry. So, tell me how Christmas was growing up with the Simmons family."

"Let's see. There was always too much food. My mom and sis loved baking. We were one of those families that opened one gift on Christmas Eve. Destiny and Braxton always tore into the biggest boxes, but me—" He changes the position of our hands so that our fingers are interlocked. "I always picked something small. Saving the best for later gave me something to look forward to. And it was always worth the wait."

There's a look in his eyes that makes my breath catch. It doesn't feel like he's just talking about Christmas presents. He's looking at me like *I'm* worth waiting for.

"And on Christmas day," he continues, like he hasn't just undone me with a look, "we'd get together and play board games once the excitement of the day wore off. We still do that now."

"What kind of games do y'all play?"

"The same ones the four of us would play during game nights with Braxton and Ivy. Spades, Uno, Charades. Last year, we got out and went to an escape room. We didn't escape in time, unfortunately." He laughs. "But it was fun. My mom was talking about doing one with you and Ivy this year."

"An escape room with me? Has your mom met me? Does she know how bossy I can get?"

"Trust, she's well aware." He squeezes my hand to soften the joke when I balk. "But she likes that about you."

I've always loved how Grant and Braxton's parents treat Ivy like she's their own, and that she's had them to lean on since losing Dad. To imagine that maybe I could have a place with them, too, feels like opening an early Christmas gift.

"So..." Grant says as we come up on the exit, glancing between it and me.

"So, I think it's about time you keep up your end of our deal and help me find a gift for your brother."

He sighs dramatically. "I mean, if you're gonna twist my arm, I guess I have no choice."

"Yeah, yeah," I say, rolling my eyes. "Come on, funny guy."

Chapter Fourteen

Some things don't change—I will forever be a Christmas Market girlie.

I'll be pushing 100, only able to get around using a walker, and I'll still rally enough energy to spend a day basking in the magic of the market.

After dragging Grant through so many booths I lost count, I found a gift for Braxton, more for Nia and Amani, and gifts for Grant's parents.

As we pull into the driveway I inhale deeply, feeling rejuvenated. Grant cuts off the engine but makes no move to get out.

"What are you doing?" I ask him.

"I can't move my legs." He turns to me, dark eyes weary and tired. "I think you broke me. So much shopping. So. Much."

"Aww, is the widdle baby tired after a few hours of walking? Did big, mean Evie keep you out past your bedtime?"

I've got to practice baby-talk somehow.

He cuts his eyes at me. "No. My back is still sore from falling off the roof, and someone had me out on the ice busting my butt."

I gasp. "I didn't even think about your fall. Are you okay? Do you need to see a doctor?"

"No doctor." A slow, sly grin transforms his face from handsome to devastating. A little *too* bright for someone supposedly unable to move. "I could use some help from the most beautiful figure skater I know though."

I don't quite trust that smile, but guilt of not thinking about his earlier injury gets me moving. I rush around the car to help him up. Even though he's got a good forty pounds on me, I grab his hands and pull with all my might. He swiftly stands up then swoops down, pressing his lips to mine in a hot, brief kiss that leaves me trying to catch my breath.

I raise my hand to my lips and scowl so I don't end up grinning like a fool. "I thought you said you needed my help."

"I did. I've been wanting to do that all day and needed your help to make it happen."

"Just for that," I say before opening the door to the backseat and pulling out a handful of shopping bags. "You get to carry these inside."

The house is warm and welcoming, working quick to thaw our frozen appendages. After setting our bags by the tree, I watch Grant stiffly take off his gloves and jacket then slip out of his shoes without using his hands. Oh yeah, he's definitely feeling the pain.

"Why don't you get cleaned up," I tell him. "I'll take care of the bags and everything else. If you need a little Bengay, let me know. I'm sure we've got some of Dad's stashed somewhere."

Once he disappears down the hall, I dash to shower and slip into holiday pajamas. By the time I'm back, Grant's still in the shower, so I set up for a gift-wrapping marathon. I get the assembly line organized with scissors, tape, paper, and bows. But something feels off.

After looking over everything, I decide it must just be me and get started.

I wrap Ivy's book reading light and some board books for the babies. When I wrap Braxton's spices, I think of how Dad would have loved testing these on some barbequed brisket and realize what's missing.

Dad's gift.

For the first time in my life, there isn't one.

The absence hits like a sudden drop in temperature. My throat tightens, my vision blurs, and the cheer drains out of me. I spent all day caught up in the Market's magic that I forgot about this holiday's largest missing piece.

How could I?

I know this is what Dad would want, but guilt, shame, and sorrow all battle to make me feel like the worst daughter.

"Are you still down here?"

I swipe at my eyes and sniff at the sound of Grant's voice.

He takes one look at me and crosses the room. "What's wrong?"

"It's stupid, but I just realized I didn't get a present for my dad." My voice wavers. "I've had all year to get used to it, but somehow it's hitting me now."

The tears spill over before I can stop them.

Grant doesn't hesitate to wrap me in his arms, and I make no attempt to fight him. I bury my face in his chest and let the grief roll through me.

"I'm sorry," I whisper once the tears slow. "We're supposed to be celebrating the season, and here I am falling apart."

Grant tilts my chin so I'm looking at him and those brown eyes full of nothing but compassion and warmth. "I never want you to apologize for missing your dad. Or for falling apart. My arms are always free for that. And actually"—his mouth lifts in a small smile as he brushes away some of my tears—"I consider it a sign of progress when you're not trying to hide your emotions from me."

"You know, you're the only man I've ever fallen apart in front of like this. Twice now."

"That tells me I must be doing something right then. And I want you to know it's an honor I don't take lightly."

In not so many words, he's telling me what I've already suspected—my heart is safe with him.

His hands slide from my back to my shoulders. "Now, I have something I want to give you."

He digs through one of his bags from the market and pulls out a small, gift-wrapped box I don't remember seeing.

"Where did that come from?" I ask.

"I got it while you were haggling with the scarf lady."

"Oh, the same scarf lady who I was able to talk down low enough to get you scarves for your whole family *and* Destiny's dog?"

I'm not about to go off again about how ridiculous it is for someone trying to oversell 'homemade' scarves they know full well they got from Temu in bulk. They were pretty enough, but nothing close in quality to the one I purchased for Grant.

Grant smirks. "That's the one."

I wipe my cheeks one more time, then make grabbing motions until Grant hands me the box.

There's barely any weight to it. I untie the red ribbon, lift the lid, and gasp. "It's a snow globe ornament."

Inside sits a tiny snow-covered house with a red truck in the driveway and snowman in the yard. When I shake it, white flakes swirl about.

"You didn't have to," I whisper.

"I know, but you love them. I saw the ones in your room and remembered how you told me you and your dad bought one every year. I thought this might help you think of the good times."

Good times. Like the year Dad, Ivy, and I built a snow-man—albeit tiny, since we'd only received an inch of snow— with our hands stuffed into two layers of Dad's thick socks because we weren't prepared for actual wintery conditions.

My eyes water again.

Grant cups my hands around the ornament so we're both holding it. "It could be the first one on the tree this year. For him."

"That would be amazing."

We approach the tree together and Grant stands back while I hang the snow globe near the top, my fingers lingering as I think of Dad.

"Lights?" Grant asks.

"Wait. Mustic first." I connect my phone to the speaker and warm, soulful Christmas tunes fill the air.

We turn off the overhead light, and when the tree lights flick on, everything glows red and gold and magic—like a scene from a Christmas picture book.

"*In my mind...*" Grant croons along to The Temptations, right on pitch.

I giggle when he reaches for the high notes. "You and those falsettos."

The smile he aims at me could melt a glacier—or the ice around my heart.

He holds out a hand and I slip mine in without hesitation. His arm slides around my waist, mine up to his shoulder, and we sway.

"Today was magical," I whisper, looking up at him. "Thank you."

"Anytime."

I rise onto my toes, brushing my lips over his in a slow, sweet kiss. And though the thought *this could be dangerous* flashes in my mind, I don't let it take root. I want Grant. The dancing, laughing, and possibility of a future.

So for once, I let joy win.

Chapter Fifteen

Three days later, Grant is still milking the fact that I fell asleep during *The Best Man: The Final Chapters*. Never mind I've seen all of the episodes. Suddenly, *he's* the expert on how the past always bleeds into the present.

"I gotta say though, Quentin's attempt to cook for Shelby reminded me of—" Grant cuts his sentence short when he finally looks back at me. He takes in my crossed arms and jutted hip and firmly closes those full lips.

"And what, exactly, did Quentin's cooking remind you of?"

Grant shrugs as he smooths the crib skirt.

"Uh huh." I lean toward the mobile. "Because for a second there, I thought you were about to say it reminded you of my stuffed shells."

"What? No, your shells were..."

"See?" I point at him. "You can't even say *good*! I'm never cooking again."

Grant grabs my hand. "There's one thing I don't play about—homemade meals. I appreciated every bite."

I scoff. I won't be mollified by his soft tone. "I thought you didn't play about pie and cracking eggs?"

"There's *three* things I don't play about: pie, cracking eggs, and homemade meals." He kisses my knuckles soft enough to make my knees wobble.

I clear my throat. "Get back to work."

"Yes, Your Honor."

We work in companionable silence, finishing the beds and slipping a cover over the nursing pillow, when the changing table catches my eye. The bins look wrong. I swap the diapers and wipes so it'll be easier for Ivy and Braxton to grab wipes with their right hand first. But when I step back, it still feels off. I adjust the wipes again so all the packet labels face the same way.

"You know Nia and Amani won't care which way the wipes face, right?" Grant teases behind me.

"They may not, but organization matters," I say primly, cheeks warming as I wonder how long he was watching.

I'm a control freak at the best of times, but those urges seem to be riding me extra today and I can't help but grab ahold of whatever is in my reach to control.

Christmas is less than two weeks away, and there's still no word about Ivy and the babies coming home. My nieces are in the NICU. My twin is in another city. And I'm here, straightening labels on wipe packs like it matters. I just feel so helpless. I can't do anything to make them stronger, can't will them into this house we've worked so hard to prepare. All I can do is wait, and waiting has never felt more unbearable in my life.

I almost ask Grant how he's holding up not being able to see everyone, but before I can he frowns.

"Do you hear that?" he asks.

I hold still, thinking for one wild second he means my racing thoughts. Then I do hear it: faint voices floating through the cold December air. Singing.

I dart to the window and press my face against the glass, unable to contain my huge smile.

"They'll be here next!" I shout like a kid who's just spotted Santa's sleigh in the sky.

Grant's behind me, trying to get a look. "Who?"

"Carolers! One of the local churches has a huge boys' youth choir they split into groups and send out to the neighborhoods." I'm already out of the nursery and heading down the stairs with Grant at my back. "They've come every year since I was a kid and I'm tellin' you, them boys can *sang*! All'um!"

It's only a matter of time before the doorbell rings, so I race for the kitchen. It's tradition to give them something as a thank you and I have just the thing in mind.

"Usually we give them candy canes," I say over my shoulder while grabbing the cookie jar. "But since we don't have any we can give them the cook—"

I freeze. The container is empty.

Now I know. I just know *this man did not.*

"Grant." I swivel, locking him in place with a glare. "What happened to the rest of the cookies?"

He swallows. "The cookies?" His eyebrows knit together like he's working on some big mystery where he's totally not the culprit.

Before I can press him, the doorbell rings.

"Carolers are here," he blurts, relief written all over his face as he tugs me toward the door.

"What? We can't open the door and offer them nothing in return for the joy they spread," I protest, digging my heels in. "There's a whole chorus in a song about it."

Grant blinks at me. "Girl, what?"

"You know—'*Now bring us some figgy pudding, now bring us some figgy pudding.*'"

Another blink. "Girl, what?"

"Ugh, it's from 'We Wish You A Merry Christmas'!"

The carolers knock again and Grant catches my hand. "Not everything requires you to give something back, Eve. Sometimes, just letting people bring you joy is enough." He looks from me to the door and patiently waits for me to make the decision.

I reach for the doorknob. As the door swings open, a harmonic *Mmm* fills the air, followed by a gorgeous swell of "Go Tell It on The Mountain." There are eight boys in ages ranging from elementary to high school with puffy jackets over matching black tuxedos. They're all so talented, so full of light, I can do nothing but stand there smiling as the blessing of Christmas drifts over us.

I smile up at Grant and he wraps his arm around my shoulders, drawing me into his side.

"Oh, I need to record some of this for Ivy," I say, grabbing my phone from my back pocket.

I manage to record a portion of them singing "Away in a Manger", and by the time they finish "O Holy Night" I'm fighting back tears.

"You were right. Those boys are good," Grant says after we wave them off and wish them a merry Christmas.

"And you were right," I say, bumping him with my shoulder. "It was nice to just enjoy their gift without rushing to give in return."

"I was right. Wow, I love those words coming from your lips," Grant says, stealing a kiss from said lips before I can cut him with my glare.

He leans back and shoots me a mischievous smile. Before he can get too far away, I grab the front of his sweater and pull him down to me for another, deeper kiss, which he eagerly returns.

It feels so right being in this man's arms. I can't believe how much I fought him before, because now I don't think I'll ever get enough of him.

My phone rings in my pocket, interrupting our little interlude.

We both groan, but I pull away anyway. "It might be Ivy."

I pull my phone out of my pocket and see it is indeed her calling.

I slide the screen to answer. "I'm switching us to video," I rush out before she can say anything. "You need to see the amazing nursery waiting for my amazing nieces."

I don't want her to see the Christmas tree yet, so I wait to hit the Facetime button until I'm jogging up the stairs.

I frown when I look at the phone, still seeing a black screen. "Did it not work? I can't see you."

Ivy sighs before her face comes into view, and my heart drops.

Chapter Sixteen

"**S**issy?" I say.

Ivy looks haggard in a way I haven't seen her since we lost Dad. Just tired and drawn, eyes swollen and nose red from crying.

My stomach cramps as my mind immediately assumes the worst. "What's wrong? Are Nia and Amani okay?"

"They're okay," she rasps, her voice raw. Then, fresh tears start rolling down her face. "Amani's still not stable enough to go home. She's getting better, but she just can't regulate her temperature. I don't know how much more of this I can take," she whispers.

All the research I did before seems to vanish and a hundred questions fly through my mind. Is it normal for babies to take this long to regulate their body temperature? What exactly are they doing to help Amani? Does this mean Nia is in the clear? Do I need to step in and talk to the nurses? The hospital director?

But going off my sister's vibe, now isn't the time to pepper her with questions. She needs encouragement.

I square my shoulders and inject as much confidence into my voice as I can. "Amani is strong. She's got Matthews' blood flowing through her. She'll be released and y'all will be home for Christmas. You'll see." And because what I really want is to see her in person, I add, "You know, I can come up there and help. The nursery is finished, and I'm almost done going through our old things. Just say the word and I'll be by your side in an instant."

Grant would probably insist on coming with me. I don't know what I'd love to see more; my nieces and Ivy, or the look on Ivy's face if Grant and I showed up together and quite a bit more friendly than what she's used to.

"No," she says, jolting me with her voice gone flat and distant. "I don't... I just don't need you here right now."

"You don't need me?" I ask slowly for confirmation that she just said what I think she just said.

She sighs. "Look, I have to go. I'll talk to you later."

She ends the call before I can get another word in, and I'm left staring at a black screen.

What just happened? Is she mad at me? Did I say the wrong thing? And what was that about her not needing me there?

"You okay?" Grant's voice is soft, but I jump anyway.

I didn't know he was behind me and don't know how much he heard.

"*I'm* okay," I lie. "Ivy though, I'm not sure what's up with her..."

I stare at the phone in my hand, ready to call her back. If there's something wrong, I need to fix it.

"She seemed pretty upset," Grant says.

"You can say that again."

Her words still echo. *I just don't need you here.*

I shove my phone in my pocket and sigh. "You know what? It's fine. She's fine. She's worried about Amani, but she'll feel better when everyone's home." I don't know if I'm trying to convince Grant or myself.

"Right," Grant says after a beat too long. But the *way* he says it, hesitant and unsure, makes my hackles rise.

"What's with that tone?"

He shakes his head and avoids my gaze.

"You've never been afraid to speak your mind around me. Don't be shy now," I urge. Maybe my tone is a little confrontational, but I'm still reeling from my disastrous talk with Ivy. I don't know what I did wrong, and now Grant wants to act funny.

He lifts one shoulder. "Maybe Ivy was looking for you to just listen. With everything going on, she probably wanted to vent. Not have you offer solutions or platitudes, or act like everything will magically be okay because 'Christmas.'"

"Because Christmas," I repeat, unbelieving.

It's not what he says, but what I know he means. That all the energy I've poured into making this holiday perfect means nothing. That Ivy doesn't need the Christmas tree, the lights, or the cookies. Or, for that matter, me.

A hot, sharp fire flares in my chest.

"First of all," I say tightly, "don't act like you know what my sister needs better than me."

"I'm not—"

"Yes. You are," I grate out. "And what? You think it's fine if she's not home for Christmas? If her and the babies have to spend their first holiday together in a hospital?"

He lifts his hands in surrender. "Whoa. This isn't court and I'm not trying to argue with you. What I'm saying is it's okay if things don't turn out how you want them to. That's it, and that's all. It doesn't mean the world is ending." His voice softens and he takes a step toward me. "But if it feels that way to you, that's okay too. I'm sorry if my words suggested otherwise."

His apology, surely meant to calm me, only grates against my skin.

"You don't get it," I snap, my voice rising. I'm not trying to yell at him, but I need to drown out the terror clawing at my throat. "I need to believe they'll be home and everything will be alright. I need you to believe it too. If you don't..." My throat closes around a knot of emotion.

My dreams of a family. Dad. Now Christmas. What's next?

"Eve—"

I hold up a hand to keep him from touching me.

"I'm tired, Grant. I'm tired of loving things that get taken away," I whisper. And I am tired. Down to my bones weary from loss after loss.

And if it's inevitably going to happen again, maybe it's better to keep the hits rolling all at once.

"You need to go," I force out.

"Go? Wait, Eve, let's talk about this."

I shake my head. "There's nothing to talk about. We had our fun, but let's be honest—this was never going to work."

His face falls. "It can if we want it to."

I wanted Dad to live a long and healthy life. I wanted to be by my sister during the most difficult time of hers.

"We don't always get what we want."

He scrubs both hands over his face. "Come on, Eve. Don't do this again. You can't push me away. Not after everything we've shared. I care about you—more than you can possibly imagine—but I can't be the only one fighting here. I'm only human. There's only so many times I can be shut out before I stop trying."

I hate the pain coating his voice.

I want to run into his arms and promise I'll do better, while another part of me wants to curl in on myself and shut the world out before it can break me again.

My emotions are a mess. And as always, when the fear gets too big, I retreat. Because as much as this hurts now, the thought of what I'll go through if I lose Grant later feels unbearable.

He reads the decision on my face and his shoulders fall. One more sigh, and he walks out the nursery.

Moments later, I hear the front door opening and closing, and his car pulling away.

This house that I've grown up in, laughed, cried, and loved in, instantly feels like a tomb without him. I wrap my arms around myself, but it does nothing to stop the chill that's already seeped in.

Chapter Seventeen

G rant doesn't come back. Not that evening or the following day. Not even to pick up his clothes and laptop.

I really did push him away for good.

So, for the next week I get what I thought I wanted all along—peace.

I use my time wisely, going all out to make the interior of the house just as decked out as the exterior. I wrap lights around the banister and decorate the mantle with garland and bows. At this point the tree is more tinsel than branches and needles, but it lights up the room. I even found the old Christmas village complete with a bookstore and post office that Ivy and I started in high school.

Everything old and unused is packed in boxes in the garage. If Ivy comes home tomorrow for Christmas, everything will be ready.

When she comes home, I correct myself, moving the final batch of shortbread cookies to a cooling rack.

A Christmas song Grant and I slow danced to starts playing from the speakers in the living room and my stomach twists. I rush to my phone and fast forward to the next song, so I don't have to think about how much I miss him.

Besides, what's done is done. I can't let myself regret ending what we had because I did it to protect myself. Life must go on, and eventually, my heart will get the message.

As the next song starts up, I hear the crunch of tires as a car approaches. My pulse leaps, only to drop when I see Ms. Thomas pulling into her driveway across the street.

I shake off the foolish disappointment that it's not… well, it doesn't matter. This is great timing anyway since I haven't given Ms. Thomas her cookies yet.

Back in the kitchen, I reach for a lower cabinet to get a storage bin, but the child lock I installed sticks. Looks like I'm keeping everybody in this house safe. The babies *and* Ivy and Braxton. At the very least, Ivy and Braxton will get a mental workout opening these things.

I'm able to slip my fingers inside to push down, then pull out with the other hand. It takes some grunting and finagling, but I finally get it open, pulling with so much force that the corner smacks my knee.

"Ahh!"

Pain explodes down my leg, sharp enough to cause my eyes to water and I drop to the ground with my knee tucked to my chest.

How is it that I've managed to turn something meant to protect into something that hurts?

I rock back and forth, but while the pain recedes, the tears don't. Even when I squeeze my eyes shut, they keep coming, hot and unrelenting.

All the planning, all the positive thinking has come down to this—an illusion of control shattered by a stupid piece of wood. Life's way of letting me know none of this was ever going to work.

Suddenly, I'm seventeen again, celebrating the word "remission" and thinking Dad still had a long life ahead of him. Monitoring his diet to ensure he did. Constantly calling while away at college then working at the firm and between caseloads to ensure he was taking his daily walks and vitamins as seriously as I took my love for him. Only to lose him in a car accident.

This time I tried to perfect Christmas, hoping that if everything was just right, Ivy would come home.

Maybe the problem isn't that I keep losing things. Maybe it's that I keep hoping I won't.

I don't know how long I sit there. Eventually the tears dry even when the ache doesn't, but I push myself up, wipe my face, and look at the cookies. It's still Christmas Eve, and I made a promise to Ms. Thomas.

Ms. Thomas's eyes go wide when she sees me standing on her porch. "Eve, what are you doing here?"

I thrust the container toward her. "I brought the cookies for you. Just like I promised!"

She blinks at them, caught off guard. "Oh, you remembered. Wonderful. I can't wait to eat them."

There's a beat of silence.

"You should have one right now," I say. "They're fresh out the oven, so it's the best time."

"Oh, I don't know about *right now* right now." Ms. Thomas lets out a nervous laugh. "I just got back from the market where you know they have so many treats and..." She trails off, eyeing me.

I try to muster a smile, but that little breakdown in the kitchen has me feeling as fragile as a glass ornament. My lower lip quivers, breath shakes with each inhale that I can't control. One wrong move, and I'm bound to shatter. I need one thing to go right. Just one. I need Ms. Thomas to eat a cookie and tell me it's the best thing she's ever tasted.

Ms. Thomas glances at the cookies again, then opens the lid. "You know what," she says softly, "I could go for something a little sweet right now."

She briefly hesitates then shoves it into her mouth with her eyes closed as if bracing for impact. I hold my breath.

Her eyes pop open and she stares at me in wonder. "Eve, these are... amazing."

A wave of relief washes over me. "Do you really like them? You promise you're not just saying that?"

"Oh no honey, I never joke about desserts." Her smile is warm and authentic. "You did an amazing job. Really."

I sniff as, once again, my emotions threaten to take over.

Ms. Thomas's eyes are full of concern. "You look like you could use a big mug of hot chocolate. Why don't you come on in, out of the cold."

I sniff again. "That sounds great."

Chapter Eighteen

When Ivy and I used to play with the neighbor-hood kids, Ms. Thomas never minded us running through her yard and driveway, but this is the first time I've actually been inside her house.

It's like stepping into a Christmas catalog. The smell of cinnamon and cloves wraps around me, easing some of the tightness in my shoulders. There's heavy burgundy curtains and velvet textures. Two narrow trees with large glittering gold ornaments flank the entryway, and a grand one in the sitting room gleams with red bows on every branch.

"Go on ahead and have a seat," Ms. Thomas says before disappearing into the kitchen.

I slide my jacket off and sink into her couch, the blanket beneath me covered in Santas of every shade. From here I can see her pouring hot chocolate into mugs from her crockpot.

I can't believe I'm here. Ms. Thomas's house was not where I imagined Christmas would take me, but the thought of going back across the street to the empty house is unbearable.

"Here, Honey." She hands me a steaming mug topped with jumbo marshmallows and cinnamon sprinkled on top.

We sit in silence for a few minutes as I sip and let the warmth and sweetness seep into my soul. For a moment, I imagine hot chocolate could fix everything wrong in my world.

Then, Ms. Thomas sets her mug on the wood coffee table and studies me. One sympathetic look is all it takes for my composure to break.

"I don't know what to do anymore." It all pours out in a rush. The stress of making everything perfect for Ivy here when I really want to be *there* for her, and how incredibly sad I am spending this Christmas without Dad.

My fight with Grant and the fear that getting too close to him would only hurt more in the long run.

My words trip over each other until I'm out of breath and not entirely sure if I'm even coherent enough for her to understand me. But when it's all out, I let out a deep, soul shuddering breath.

Ms. Thomas studies me for a long moment, then quietly says, "You remind me of your father."

I smile weakly. "Because I'm a control freak?"

"Because you love so fiercely," she says gently. "He did too. But he gave so much of himself to others that he forgot to leave anything for his own happiness."

I glance down. She's not wrong. Dad's life revolved around Ivy and me. Of course, as we got older, we encouraged him to branch out with hobbies and even find love, but he claimed to be content with raising us. I've often wondered if that was truly the case.

"I guess you knew him pretty well," I say, some of my misgivings seeping into my voice.

"Make no mistake, you and Ivy were his life. I don't think he had any regrets for devoting everything he could to raising you two into the beautiful women that you are. It's just that after your mother passed, it took him a long time to open his heart again. But once he did... that is to say your dad and I..." Ms. Thomas takes a long sip of her hot chocolate and lets out a nervous laugh. "Whew, I should've gone with the eggnog." I watch her through narrowed eyes as she finally takes a deep breath and squares her shoulders. "Well, we were together for a while. Romantically."

My mouth falls open. "I'm sorry, come again. You and... *my* daddy?"

I've never seen Ms. Thomas blush but blush she does.

"It wasn't long. We grew close after you and your sister left for college." She shrugs like it's no big deal, but when she drops her eyes and stares into her cup, memories play behind her eyes. "He was a good man, Eve. And even though he was by no means *old*, he did wish he made time for love earlier in his life. The fear of losing someone again the way he did your mother kept him emotionally paralyzed for years."

My throat tightens, but I can picture it. Ms. Thomas stopping by with the extra food she "just happened" to make, and Dad softening from polite acceptance to quietly looking forward to her drop-ins. Whenever we'd talk on the phone, he certainly never seemed to mind when he'd mention her meals. I should have picked up that something was going on then. I didn't, but the thought of him finding comfort with her makes my heart ache in the best way.

"We may not have had long with one another, but what we had was special," Ms. Thomas says wistfully. "I cherish every second I spent with him." She lays a hand on my arm and squeezes softly. "You have his big heart, Eve. He would want you to use it, not protect it so fiercely that you forget how to."

When I leave, the windy air doesn't bite quite as sharply. My chest feels lighter, like I can finally take that much needed deep breath. I know I won't forget her words for a long time. Now, whether I'll apply her lesson to my own life remains to be seen.

And then I *see* it. The lights are on at my house.

I pause right outside of Ms. Thomas's door. I know I hadn't turned on the Christmas lights before I left, and Grant was never able to get the timer to work.

Grant? Is he back?

My pulse leaps, but when I reach the driveway, it's not his sedan I see. It's Ivy's.

Chapter Nineteen

I'm across the street and bursting into the house in a flash.

"Ivy!" I yell as the door swings shut behind me.

There's a small crash from the kitchen and a gasped, "Eve?"

I sprint toward the sound and find Ivy standing next to the counter over a plate of dropped cookies.

We both squeal as I rush forward and wrap her up in the biggest embrace. She's warm and solid, and my heart is so full as we rock back in forth after what feels like forever.

Once we've finally gotten our fill, we lean back with our arms still linked, far enough to see each other but not ready to let go.

"What arc you doing here?" I blurt as Ivy asks, "Where have you been?"

"The decorations look amazing. I had no idea you were doing all of this," Ivy says while I tell her, "I just got back from Ms. Thomas's house. Did you know her and Dad were an item?"

"I missed you so much!" we end up saying in perfect sync.

"Copy!" Ivy fires out.

"Ugh! Paste."

We erupt into giggles and hug again.

"Okay, okay," I say, trying to get ahold of myself. It's hard to do when shocks of elation course through my body like electricity.

My cheeks hurt from how wide my smile is as I look my sister over, taking stock of her red sweater dress and favorite fur lined boots. Her eyes are bright with happiness and her skin glows. The most notable difference, of course, is her flatter stomach.

I can't believe she's standing in front of me.

"What are you doing here?" I ask.

"Amani was finally released a few days ago. I'm telling you Eve, it was like a miracle. One day they were saying it'd possibly be another couple of weeks before she was strong enough, then out of nowhere she made a total turnaround. Braxton's parents wanted us to stay with them throughout Christmas, but I had the feeling you needed me here more."

A knot of emotion is stuck in my throat and all I can do is nod.

"And, wow, Sissy. The woman that you are...I cannot believe everything you did here." Ivy's gaze sweeps from the kitchen and into the living room. "The lights. The tree. And my gosh, you seriously found our janky little

Christmas village and made it shine. And the cookies? I was on my third helping." She laughs, shaking her head. "I can't thank you enough for it all."

I almost mention how I was only able to do it with Grant's help, but his name gets stuck in my throat. I don't know if Grant told Braxton anything about us, and I don't want to ruin this moment by telling Ivy how I pushed him away after all.

Before I have to say anything, a small cry slices through the silence. I turn and see Braxton coming forward while gently rocking a tiny bundle side to side.

"Someone's hungry," he says, voice warm.

Ivy immediately holds her hands out. "Come here, Sunshine."

Braxton hands over his treasure then immediately wraps me in a bear hug.

"Thank you, Eve. Thank you so much for everything you've done for us. I know I said it a million times already, but it still doesn't feel like enough." He places a soft kiss on my forehead.

I never realized how similar in stature he and Grant are. I'll forever love Braxton for how much he loves my sister and now my nieces, but his hug reminds me of how much I miss Grant's arms around me. Grant's hugs, gentle and unwavering, felt like being encased in love.

"Do you want me to make her a bottle?" Braxton asks Ivy.

Ivy shakes her head. "No. We haven't unpacked the formula yet, and this little one is ready to go feral." The baby in her arms turns toward Ivy's clothed chest with her mouth open, reminding me of a nesting baby bird waiting for food to magically appear in their open beaks. "I'll go upstairs and nurse her."

Ivy beams at me. "My milk came in! My supply is still low so thank God the nurses supplied me with a few cans of formula. These babies can eat."

As if the baby in her arms understands what Ivy's saying, she butts Ivy's chest even more and lets out a frustrated cry.

"Okay, okay," Ivy coos. "Let's get you fed."

I follow Ivy upstairs and into the nursery where she gets settled in the rocking chair with the baby and nursing pillow. Framed by the window and low light from the hallway, this scene is exactly how I imagined it would be.

I quietly move to the crib holding the still sleeping baby.

"Who is who?" I whisper.

"You're looking at Amani. And this is Nia."

My gaze lingers on sweet sleeping Amani. She's swaddled in a pink blanket with a knitted red and white cap on, so all I see is her angelic face. Her complexion is a light golden brown a few shades lighter than both Ivy and Braxton, making me wonder when her melanin will bloom. And her lips are the perfect little bow shape.

"You can pick her up," Ivy encourages.

I hesitate, not wanting to wake her, but ultimately my need to finally hold her wins out. I gently scoop her from the crib and position her carefully in my arms. She doesn't so much as stir.

"Ivy, you made a whole baby," I whisper, looking down at my perfect niece, marveling at how light and warm she feels in my arms.

"Well, I had some help."

I glance up to find the smirk I heard in Ivy's voice.

"And, I think you mean I made *two* whole babies," she corrects.

"Do you think Nia told her little sister to get better so y'all could come home?"

There's the sound of rustling clothes before Ivy comes to stand beside me. "If she's anything like *my* big sister, she was rallying her and encouraging her the whole time."

We face each other. Twins holding twins. This is all I wanted, yet my heart in no way feels whole. There are too many missing pieces.

"Dad would have loved seeing us like this," Ivy says on a sigh. "And he would have made a great grandpa."

No surprise that our thoughts, as always, align.

"He would have," I say.

We don't need to say more. Our grief is the same, but so are our memories of him. I know that beneath Ivy's ache flows the same deep current of love, laughter, and joy that shaped me into the woman I am today. This Christmas hurts without him here, but his love still lingers, wrapping around us like a quiet blessing.

After a while, Amani wakes to be fed then both babies are sleeping again. Ivy and I stand at the window, gazing into the kind of quiet only felt the night before Christmas.

"Braxton's parents are coming tomorrow," Ivy tells me. "I hope you don't mind."

"Of course not. They're your family and this is your house now, remember?"

"I know I live here now, but this will always be your home too. You have just as much history here as me." Identical eyes lock on mine. "I swear this year tried to do me in. Losing Dad, getting pregnant right after the wedding, moving while pregnant. And you've been right here through it all, keeping me sane and encouraged." She frowns. "I can't help but wonder if maybe I leaned on you too much."

"Ivy, I'm your big sister. Being here for you to lean on is my job."

"You're eight minutes older and a quarter of an inch taller. When will you let it go?"

"When you magically become taller and older than me." I give her a look that says *duh*, and her eyes promise retribution.

"What I'm trying to say is that it goes both ways. You don't have to carry everything on your own. You've got family to lean on, and a home open to you whenever you need it. Always." She heaves a heavy sigh. "For the record, even though you're barely older than me—I will always need my big sister around."

I lay my head on her shoulder, careful not to jostle either of the babies.

Ivy hums a sweet tune to fill the silence.

"Braxton spoke to Grant while we were driving home," she says after a while. "Apparently, he's back in San Antonio and is going to try and catch a last-minute flight to see Destiny tomorrow instead of coming to meet the most beautiful babies in the world. Is there something you need to tell me?"

This should be the part where I finally confess all—that holding everything together has felt impossible at times, while other times the fear of losing more people I love threatens to crush me. And despite it all, Grant somehow slipped under my defenses, filled the cracks and made me whole.

But the words lodge in my throat. So, knowing she's going to kill me later, I shake my head. "Not yet."

Car headlights blend with Christmas lights as Ms. Thomas pulls into her driveway. She gets out of the car with an armful of shopping bags likely from the Christmas Market.

"I can't believe her and Dad had a secret romance," Ivy says. Then softer, "I'm glad he had her."

"Me too."

"And I know it's not the same, but I'm glad you had Grant with you this past month. Even if you won't tell me what happened. I'm bummed to have missed all of our Christmas traditions, but at least you weren't alone."

The relief of having Ivy home fades as a weight presses in on me. *I had Grant.* And I pushed him away.

I think about how he admitted the loneliness of keeping himself apart from his family after leaving the NBA, and his vow to do better. To show up for them. For me. My stomach twists now thinking of how he's currently alone instead of spending time with his brother and nieces after all the hard work he put into the house, while I'm here surrounded by love. Nothing about this is right.

And just like that, a plan forms.

"There is one tradition we can do together," I tell Ivy, already thinking up my new list.

Ivy gasps. "That's right! Our Christmas Eve movie. How could I forget? Let's put Nia and Amani down and watch it before it gets too late."

"Wait." I look down at my niece and my heart melts all over again. "Can we bring them? I need to make up for lost cuddles."

"Of course."

Ivy and I go downstairs, settling onto the couch with the babies nestled close. *The Preacher's Wife* starts up as Braxton joins us, kissing Ivy, kissing his daughters, and sliding right into the warmth of our little circle.

I soak it all in while I can. Love, family, Christmas magic. And tomorrow, I'll make everything right.

Chapter Twenty

It's a Christmas miracle. Snow in central Texas.

Really, it's more of a dusting—melting the moment it lands on your palm—but by the time I pull into Grant's driveway, it coats the rooftops like powdered sugar and makes everything sparkle.

The only thing breaking the peace is my phone buzzing nonstop in the cup holder. Ivy's name flashes across the screen again. She found my note under the tree, which means she's currently alternating between worrying and dreaming up different ways to strangle me.

I'll deal with apologizing to her later. For now, I have another apology I need to make.

I place a hand on my stomach and let out a deep breath to ease the knot of nerves. I can do this. I just need to act like I'm in court.

I cut off the engine, grab the letter waiting in my passenger's seat, and march to the door before I can talk myself out of it. When I ring the bell, I instantly regret not changing into something more put-together. Jeans and boots aren't exactly something I'd wear to court. Maybe I should run to the gas station, change, and come back—

The door opens, and it's too late.

"Eve?"

Just hearing Grant's voice makes my whole being yearn. Seeing him makes me ache. While it's still early morning, he's dressed in jeans, a soft gray sweater, and the scarf I got him from the market.

I want to reach out, grip that scarf, and kiss him, but the guarded look in his eyes keeps me from acting on the impulse.

Instead, I square my shoulders and lift the letter. "Grant, hi. Good morning, er, that is Merry Christmas. I came to give you this."

He frowns. "Am I being served?"

"No! I would never." He lifts one eyebrow and I shrug. "I mean, I *would*, but that's not what this is."

He finally takes it, gently unfolding it to read its contents. Meanwhile, I can barely breathe. My stomach twists a little more with each second he stays silent.

When he finally looks up, his expression is unreadable. "Eve. What is this?"

"It's a custody agreement." His eyebrows shoot up, and I rush on before he can say anything. "It's my plan to make everything up to you. You get to celebrate every holiday and birthday with Braxton and Ivy for the next two years—except Nia and Amani's first birthday, obviously. I mean, I am a first-time aunt. After that though, we'll split them evenly, alternating every year."

I stop talking, though my pulse thuds in my ears. He's studying me and I can't read a single thing in his normally expressive face.

"A custody agreement," he says slowly. "For two grown adults."

"And their kids," I add weakly.

His mouth twitches, but he schools it quickly.

He looks down at the paper again, shakes his head, and huffs out something between disbelief and laughter. "You came all the way here to tell me you want to trade off birthdays, Christmas, New Year's, even Juneteenth, like we're divorced parents?"

"That's exactly what I did, because you deserve to be able to show up for your family without my hindrance." I pause, my heart thumping wildly. This doesn't feel right. "But now that I'm here, I realize it's not what I want. I didn't come because of some agreement. I came because I miss you. I came, because I was wrong to push you away."

In the stretching silence, his eyes soften.

Finally, Grant steps back, opening the door wider. "Come inside before you freeze."

I step over the threshold and into Grant's home.

He closes the door, leaning against it with a sigh. "I knew you were going to do this."

I eye him. He's so handsome it should be illegal. "Do what?"

"Realize you were pushing me away because you were scared, then try to make it right by sacrificing yourself in some overcomplicated gesture." He holds up the paper with a smirk. "Like drafting a custody agreement instead of just saying you're sorry."

I don't know whether to be offended or amused. He knows me so well. "You're unbelievable."

He balls up the paper and tosses it toward his open office. It lands perfectly in the wastebasket.

"Nothing but net," I mutter.

"Nothing but net," he echoes, closing the distance between us. "You don't have to trade holidays with me, Eve. You just need to stop running."

"I'm trying," I say, my voice cracking on a sudden swell of emotion. He's so close to being mine again I can't take it.

"I know you are." He steps closer, his hand finding my cheek, warm and sure.

I step into his warmth. "So don't give up on me. Please."

His thumb traces my cheek, slow and tender while he wraps his free hand around my waist. "I won't. I can't." A self-deprecating laugh. "I've tried. You're stubborn, and a control freak, and you drive me up the wall the way you try to take the world on your shoulders. But I have been in love with you since the minute I saw you. And every moment that we've spent together has felt like a gift."

I lean into his touch and close my eyes, reveling in his words. The feeling he gives me—butterflies, hope, joy—all wrapped with a bow.

I didn't think I'd ever feel this way again. Not after losing so much and convincing myself that kind of happiness was for other people. But Grant changed that. He made me believe in the possibility of family again, of laughter in a kitchen, of a future filled with more than memories and grief.

This must have been what Dad felt when he let himself love Ms. Thomas. Standing here with Grant, I believe every single one of Ms. Thomas's words—this is what Dad wanted for me. To open my heart and let love in.

I slide my hands over Grant's chest and around his neck. Standing on my toes, I breathe him in, noticing the slight smile across his lips. "I love you too."

And then we're kissing. It's slow and sweet, full of promises and love.

"You taste sweet," I say when we pull apart.

"I just had some hot cocoa," he says. "You can have some if you want."

"It's about time you offered to share."

"If you wanted some, that's all you had to say. Because there's one thing I don't play about—"

"Let me guess," I say. "Hot chocolate?"

He kisses the tip of my nose. "Nope. You."

I don't try hiding my goofy smile.

Grant grabs my hand and pulls me toward the kitchen. "Come on. I'll make you a cup and then we need to head out."

"Head out? Where?"

"Back to Ivy and Braxton's. Ivy's been blowing up my phone all morning and wondering where you are. I'm not going to repeat the threats she made, but I never realized how scary she is."

"That, she is."

Chapter Twenty-One

Grant and I drive the whole way back holding hands and singing Christmas songs, and two hours later we're back at my childhood home.

When we pull up to the house, Grant kisses my knuckles before we walk up to the door.

"You know I have a key right?" I say after he knocks.

He grins and threads his fingers through mine. "I know, but it'll be better this way."

The door opens and Ivy, dressed in Rudolph pajamas, glares at me. "I cannot believe you took off like that! Do you know how it felt to wake up and find nothing but that stupid note? I swear, if you weren't my twin, I would—"

She cuts off with a gasp when her eyes drop to my hand in Grant's.

I smile at Grant before unlocking our fingers and stepping forward to wrap Ivy in a hug. "Merry Christmas."

Her arms are slow to come around me, but when they do, she holds on just as tight, whispering to me hotly, "I swear if you don't tell me everything the second the babies are down and the movie is on, I *will* embarrass you in front of everyone."

"I will. I swear."

I raise my pinky. She hooks hers around mine with a satisfied nod. The tight knot in my chest unwinds.

I hug Braxton, his parents, even Ms. Thomas, then gather Nia and Amani in my arms, soaking up their snuggles in matching *My First Christmas* onesies.

When it's time to pass out presents, Grant tugs me down beside him. His arm stays anchored around me, his warmth steady and sure. He doesn't want to let me out of his sight, and I have no plans on pushing him away. Now or ever.

Grant leans in, his lips brushing mine as he murmurs, "Merry Christmas, Eve."

The End

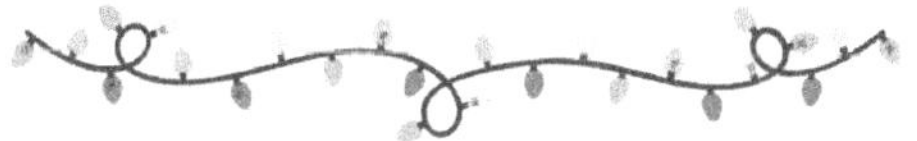

About the author

Etta Easton is a certified hopeless romantic who now writes contemporary romance. Her stories are full of humor, relatable heroines, swoonworthy heroes, and Black joy. She lives in Central Texas with her husband and two young kids.

Learn more about her at http://www.EttaEaston.com

Also by Etta Easton

The Kiss Countdown
The Love Simulation